Farewell,

Frank Merriwell

BY

GEORGE ZUCKERMAN

E. P. DUTTON & CO., INC · NEW YORK · 1973

also by George Zuckerman

THE LAST FLAPPER

for
SARAH MILLER ZUCKERMAN
and
DAVID ZUCKERMAN

FIRST EDITION

Published simultaneously in Canada by
Clarke, Irwin & Company Limited, Toronto and Vancouver
SBN: 0-525-10345-7
Library of Congress Catalog Card Number: 74-179847

Saturday, June 1, 1968

ONE

The train was in the tunnel before Forrest Devers raised *The New York Times*. The body type a blur, he blamed the midnight hour, the whiskey, and the Long Island Rail Road before he remembered to use his reading glasses.

The blur was gone, the *Times* was gone. He beheld in his hands the dead *World-Telegram*. Eyes shut, he stilled his heart and tried again. The alive *Times*. KENNEDY in a one-column headline. Dateline San Francisco. From San Francisco he fled to Dallas. From Bobby he fled to Jack. Alive.

Devers dropped the newspaper and shut his eyes to read his column in the last edition of the *World Journal Tribune*, a too brief candle from the tallow of his own *World-Telegram*, the *Journal American*, and the *Herald Tribune*.

The column had ended with a poem. "Between the crosses row on Park Row . . ." He could recall no more, save a reference to Frank Munsey and Frankenstein.

He tried to remember the poem he had written the day Arlington's earth turned for Jack. Neither the words nor the place where the copy paper was hidden appeared to him.

Devers was quick to blame the boy unable to accept the death of things—the boy hiding within him.

"What's the use of being a boy if you're going to grow up to be a man?"

A question, a reproach voiced by an old man who had

trained one of the three-year-olds entered in the Belmont Stakes. It had chased Devers from 33 West 52nd Street to Penn Station.

Turning to the train window, the lean man in the coconut straw searched his reflection for the boy hiding within him. He saw his father's face, the lights beyond the tracks, the distress signals.

At Valley Stream Devers quit the train. Blind to the familiar, he found the Thunderbird and the mile home. Twentieth-century magic raised the garage door, but it took a worn key and a tired hand to open the white front door of the low-swept Colonial house.

The door to the master bedroom was shut. The doors to two vacant bedrooms were open. He put out the lamp in the living room and took the dark through the dining room, the tavern kitchen, and the breezeway leading to the hideaway.

Redwood beams. Bookshelves holding millions of words about Frank and Dick Merriwell, about American battlegrounds and playing fields. Desk, ancient Remington portable, whiskey drawer, radio-phonograph, records, convertible sofa, leather chair, and high sliding windows to foil the boy hiding within Devers. The sleeprunner.

On the wall abutting the desk a framed photograph: two faces. One glance sent Devers into drawers, books, albums, and memory for the lost poem.

The search failing, Devers showered but did not sing, made his bed, music, and dark. He was awake when the telephone rang.

He came off the bed alert for a fresh bulletin on the death of things. His voice was raspy. "Hello."

"Dad?"

His daughter's voice, wary and tense, confirmed his fears. "Donna! How are you?"

"I'm fine. And you?"

"I feel great."

"I hear Robert Goulet. Did I wake you?"

"No. Hold it a second while I turn down the—"

"Don't, Dad. The music might help."

"Donna, where are you?"

"Santa Barbara."

"Santa Barbara? Did Bavasi send you down?"

"Dad, I don't get it."

"The Dodgers have a farm club in Santa Barbara."

"Yes, Dad," she said with laughter.

"So what's a nice girl like you doing in a place like Santa Barbara?"

Devers heard no more laughter, only a sickening pause followed by a subdued voice. "Good question. Ready for a curve, Dad?"

He was anything but ready. The pitch struck his head and he fell as Ray Chapman had fallen. He arose quickly and laughed quickly. "I hit curves better than Ted Williams ever did. Throw it."

He heard his daughter take a deep breath, exhale, and say, "I'm Mrs. Herbert Mouritzen."

"Mrs. Herbert Mouritzen! Sure, that's the name of the heroine in Ibsen's play. *The Dog House*." He laughed to forget his nausea. "Right?"

"You might be at that," she said sadly.

"Donna, feed me another straight line."

"How do you spell 'Mouritzen'?"

"Mouritzen of Harvard?"

"The same."

"Good for you, Mrs. Herbert Mouritzen. That's great news. When did it happen?"

"Thanks, Dad. I love you."

"I love you, fatbelly."

"Do you forgive me?"

"Forgive you? For what? For interrupting the turning of the earth to bring me a very special announcement that love has found Donna Devers?"

"I did break my promise."

Devers decided to be as dumb as Fred Merkle. "What promise?"

"Come on, Dad, you never forget anything."

Making light of the heavy, he asked, "Then how come I can't remember where I put that Pulitzer-prize poem I wrote the night Kennedy was buried? How come I can't recall a single line of the greatest poem written since Browning went on to invent the automatic rifle?"

Mrs. Herbert Mouritzen did not laugh as Donna Devers might have laughed. "Dad, I don't believe you."

"I swear it. Do you remember the poem?"

"You never showed it to me." When he said nothing, she added, "I was only fifteen."

Devers' laughter sounded canned to him. "That explains it. You were on the telephone from fifteen to eighteen. And now you're twenty and breaking promises. Hey, did the bridegroom break the glass?"

She broke into his fresh laughter. "In a civil ceremony performed in the Santa Barbara municipal building."

"Was Miles the best man?"

"No."

Returning his son to San Francisco, he plunged into the middle of the line. "Fatbelly, what promise did you break to me?"

"Dad, I'm twenty and I'm married."

"You hardly qualify as child bride of the year."

"Please, Dad."

He gave it a second effort. "What the hell! I'm sure Judge Oscar Farrell is just as good a judge as Mark O'Neal."

"Dad, we'll be home tomorrow night."

"Great! We'll roll out the red-eye."

"And we'll be leaving Sunday night for Washington."

Forsaking jokes about Johnson and the White House, he solemnly asked, "Can we unbreak your promise?"

"How?"

"How about if we throw you a wedding reception Sunday afternoon?"

"Dad, you don't have time to—"

"Sure, I do. I'll call Jack Fallon. He can bring it off. Just some of our friends and relations, your friends, Herb's friends. Just want to show you off, just a bash. Look, I'll invite Judge O'Neal. Have to. He's been looking forward to kissing the bride. Okay?"

"Hadn't you better talk to mother?"

"You talk to her. Just hold—"

"Dad! This *is* my wedding night."

"Call your mother in the morning. Please. By the way, where are you staying?"

"The Santa Barbara Biltmore."

"Nice hotel. I'll see you at Kennedy."

Devers overheard a male dissent before Donna responded. "We'll take a taxi. You'll be busy enough."

"Good thinking. What does Herb drink?"

"Tanqueray. On the rocks."

"Good. Look, fatbelly, tell Herb something for me. Tell him I give him my love. See you tomorrow."

"Goodbye, Dad."

"And a very good night to you, Mrs. Mouritzen!"

Remaining at his desk, Devers took two shots of Wild Turkey and smoked one cigarette before he touched his own cold sweat on the telephone.

He remembered the San Francisco area code and nothing more. Slamming down the telephone, he found his blue book and the number he should not have forgotten. While he waited for the magic of circuits, he damned Walter O'Malley for stealing the Dodgers and his daughter, Horace Stoneham for stealing the Giants and his son.

He wearied of the ringing and the waiting to hear his son's voice. No answer. He tried again and again. No magic, no San Francisco, no Miles. He could not understand it. The earthquake had hit far to the south.

TWO

The ghosts led Devers through the dark house to the master bedroom. He rapped and heard nothing. He opened the door and heard panic. Mag feared he was sick and dying.

He was. But he was John McCormack singing a glad song about Santa Barbara, Donna, and Herbert Mouritzen. The last name was a problem in spelling and memory.

Miles' letters from Harvard. The physics professor—the *young* physics professor who took such an interest in him, who tried to convert him from mathematics to physics, who became one of his friends. A brilliant man, a brilliant, *young* man. Probably in his early thirties now. From Wisconsin. His parents on the University of Wisconsin faculty. A Swedish name. Probably Lutherans.

Mag was forlorn. Were the postmen on strike? The telephone lines down? Why the surprise? Why the secret? Why did Donna call her father? Why did Donna keep her in the dark? She thought the worst. Donna was pregnant. Herbert was a dirty old man.

She cared not that the Mouritzens were coming to Valley Stream Saturday night. She opposed Devers' plans for a Sunday afternoon wedding reception. She refused to telephone her sisters in South Carolina. What invitation? What celebration?

Devers was patient and understanding. After a while she was reassured. Yes, she wanted her sisters to be here. Yes, Jack Fallon could cater such an affair on short notice. She could do it. She was almost smiling when she looked at Devers and began to weep.

"You may have a funeral Sunday," she said.

Devers said nothing. He braced himself for another round of melancholia.

"Karen collapsed. Yesterday. Friday."

Devers groaned and damned himself for believing he was the one who was sick and dying. Karen was his sister. For forty-six of her forty-eight years she had been an invalid.

"She's in the infirmary," Mag said. "Sister Alicia telephoned late this evening. I told her you'd be there in the morning."

"I'll be there," he said to the death of things.

"Karen always frightened me. Nuns—"

"Good night, Mag."

She detained him. An idle question about breakfast. Devers knew what he wanted: a large bowl of oatmeal swimming in sweet butter and sweet cream, a fresh bagel swollen with butter and cream cheese and a cup of hot chocolate with whipped cream floating on top of the whiteness and warmth of his mother's kitchen, with Karen smiling across the table from him. He requested bacon and eggs and tried to leave the bedroom.

Mag called his name. He stopped.

"How did Donna sound?"

"Very happy." He did not stir. He heard the death rattle on Staten Island before he heard Mag again.

"My God, the stainings, the morning sicknesses, the nightmares of miscarriages. How she rushed to be born, and how happy I was to have a girl. I so wanted a daughter, she so wanted me. For a year—when she was two—I carried her again. In my lap. She clung to me so. She wept so when I had to be out of her sight. How I loved life, how I loved her."

Mag wept. Devers left. He did not want her to say more, he did not want to hear more.

Unable to make it past his daughter's room, he entered and allowed memory to light the darkness: the design of the wallpaper, the designs of the wallpapers laminated by an artless time that had changed a crib into a pair of studio beds, a linoleum into a fluffy carpet, dolls into Beatles, Nancy Drew into Madame Bovary, a Camp Tioga banner into a UCLA banner, and Donna Devers into Mrs. Herbert Mouritzen.

Drawn deeper into the room, Devers sat down on the window seat and played with a doll purchased in Augusta and costumed as an antebellum Southern belle. It reminded him of Mag, the girl with the cornsilk hair. He stayed with the memory until Staten Island took him. When he arose, he brushed a tense hand against a bronze giraffe. It fell and struck a ceramic ashtray on the desk.

Devers waited for Mag to come running. The ghost of his mother-in-law came out of the closet before he fled to his hideaway, to a magic circuit that brought San Francisco within the range of his desperation.

THREE

He heard a girl laughing, a sweet hello.

"Is Miles there, please?"

"Who's calling?"

He told her.

"Oh, Mr. Devers! Hello! I'm Shelley."

"You sound more like Elizabeth Barrett Browning."

This time the laughter was meant for him. "Very good. I'm looking forward to meeting you, Mr. Devers."

"Likewise."

"Here's Milo."

The next voice Devers heard was dead. "Dad, how are you?"

"Fine, Miles, and you?"

"I'm pissed off. How's Mom taking it?"

"You know, huh?"

"I introduced the prick to my stupid sister."

"I seem to remember you writing letters home about what a great guy Professor Mouritzen was."

"Dad, when did I stop writing letters home?"

"In your junior year."

"Let me bring you up to date. My *brother-in-law* is a supercilious prick."

"How do you explain it?"

"The marriage?"

"Yeah."

"I can't."

"What's Mouritzen of Harvard doing in California?"
"Hastening the end of the world."
"English translation?"
"He's been with the Rand Corporation for almost two years now."
Devers understood. "I take it he's a hawk."
"A hawkish prick."
"Miles, aren't you shocking Shelley?"
"She's a Radcliffe girl."
"*Your* girl?"
"One of my girls. Any more questions about Mouritzen?"
"How old is he?"
"Thirty-seven."
"Jesus!"
"What the hell could I do? He called me one night around Easter and said he'd like to drop by for a drink."
"Tanqueray."
"Beg your pardon."
"Herb drinks Tanqueray gin. Donna told me."
"Not in my place. And I'll tell you something else, Dad. He doesn't like to be called 'Herb.' "
"Thanks for warning me. What else should I know?"
"I was trying to tell you how he met Donna."
"I'm listening."
"Donna flew up here for a weekend. She was here when *Herbert* showed up."
"Love at first sight?"
"You kidding? It was a scene from the theater of the absurd. I had to kick the prick out."
His own voice dead now, Devers asked, "What was he doing?"
"He was bitchy."
"Has he been married before?"
"No. But, anticipating your next question, no, he's not a

fag. One of the reasons he left Harvard for Rand was that he was balling some instructor's wife."

"Decent chap."

"I'm sick about it. How the hell did I know that the prick would return to Santa Monica and start romancing Donna?"

"It's a short ride to Westwood."

"Donna loves Herbert. Herbert loves Donna. End of tragedy."

"Why didn't you go to Santa Barbara?"

"I wasn't asked. I was told, after the fact."

"Would you have gone if invited?"

"No, Dad, I'm too busy. Between Berkeley and *Ramparts*—shit!"

"How does it look for Bobby?"

"Another Kennedy murdered. In Oregon, by McCarthy," said Miles without emotion.

"The polls have Bobby leading in California."

"He'll win California on Tuesday. He'll lose Chicago to Humphrey."

"Can I ask you a favor?"

"What is it?"

"Fly home tomorrow night. Fly back Sunday night." Silence. "We're having a bash for Donna."

"Sorry—"

"I'll pick up the tab."

"I know that."

"It's not for me. Not for your mother. Not for Herbert. Only for Donna. Do you understand me?"

"Yes, Dad, but I can't make it. I'll call home Sunday afternoon. I'll talk to Donna and to Mom. And to Herbert."

"And what are you going to tell Herbert?"

"Exactly what you want me to tell him."

"What did Rogers Hornsby bat in 1924?"

Without hesitation, Miles said, ".424."

"You haven't forgotten."

"I read Forrest Devers five days a week."

"You people in San Francisco sure know how to live."

"Dad, when are you coming out this way again?"

"Soon." His voice was choked. "I'll make it soon."

"Dad?" A note of concern.

"Yeah, Miles."

"What did Joe Jackson bat in 1911?"

"Jesus! I can't remember!"

"You're putting me on."

"No. Miles, what did Joe Jackson bat in 1911?"

".408."

"Yeah."

"Dad, are you all right?"

The timbre returned to Devers' voice. "I'm fine. I'm glad about forgetting what I should've forgotten long ago. I am." Silence. "Miles, do you remember the poem I wrote the night Kennedy was buried?"

"I was at Harvard. I never saw it."

"Listen, Miles. Tell me if this is a quote: 'What's the use of being a boy if you're going to grow up to be a man?' "

Miles did not know. Shelley did.

Devers laughed and the last thing he told his son was how he had been chased from Toots Shor's by Gertrude Stein.

Soon, in a darkness of his own choosing, Devers was lying in bed and listening to his John McCormack records. The songs of sentiment carried him back to a night in 1915 when the Irish tenor sang in the Hippodrome, when happenstance seated together in the balcony Thomas Aquinas Devers and Miriam Wald.

He went back to 1955, to the Holy Name Cemetery, to hear his father's lament: "The night I left the Hippodrome with Miriam I thought it would all go on forever."

And the remembrance of his retort to the open grave came back to haunt him: "It does. In the dust."

1955 to 1964, dust to dust, grave beside grave, Tom and Miriam, forever.

McCormack sang, Devers sang.

Farewell, Joe Jackson, I lost my heart in Santa Barbara. Hail, Forever. Whisper to me, free me from the boy hiding within me.

FOUR

His heart and head heavy, Devers tried to hold down his bacon and eggs as he listened to Mag's morning lament. Charlie Spencer worried her. She bled for him, but she could not endure Charlie's drinking, his foul mouth, and his degeneration into a dirty old man. She was afraid to think of what he might do at the reception. She begged Devers not to invite Charlie.

He said nothing. He would concern himself with Charlie later. Now he wanted only to occupy himself with the girl who had never run, skipped rope, danced, or been kissed by a boy. She was always "Karen" to him, never "Sister Antonia."

At a shopping center in Valley Stream he stopped to buy a dozen white roses, a five-pound box of Barton's chocolates, and a copy of François Mauriac's *The Inner Presence.*

The death of things fled before the vista of the Verrazano Bridge only to return with the sight of the convent walls.

As he passed through the cloistered garden beyond the colonnades, he had no eyes for Christ or for St. Thérèse of Lisieux. He did match smiles with the novice who guided him to the infirmary and to the gray room where his sister lay abed.

Devers tried to see Karen as the stricken girl confined to a well-remembered bed from which she had a window view of the dance of life on a Bay Ridge street. But he saw her as time had tampered with her: the pallor as gray as the stucco walls and the blanket; the death mask jeweled with clear, blue-gray eyes that saw the life of things; the thin, pale hands bound by prayer beads.

They gave smiles to each other. Her fingers touched his face and he touched her fingers with his lips. He sat down in the straight oak chair and she spoke to him in a voice that had a sweeter tinkle than the small silver bell resting upon the night table.

With a child's pleasure Karen opened and examined her presents. After the novice had departed with the flowers and the candy, the patient blessed the book with her beads and beat the visitor to solicitude.

She recalled the day she heard mother reply to a concerned neighbor: "The well one is well, the sick one is sick." Now Karen wished to know if *the well one* was, indeed, well.

When Devers told her he was running at Belmont this afternoon, she wished for a subscription to a newspaper carrying his column, and for a funny story. He pleased her with the Hartford *Courant,* but not with his funny story about Santa Barbara.

Karen produced a telegram from under her pillow. Devers read: "YOU ARE THE FIRST TO KNOW. BECAME MRS. HERBERT MOURITZEN TODAY. REMEMBER I LOVE YOU. PLEASE PRAY FOR ME." When he looked up, Karen's smile said all that needed to be said about Santa Barbara. Now she prompted him for the funny story.

Devers hesitated until he remembered the French word for the Anglo-Saxon punch line. He told her a golf story about a priest and a nun. When the priest topped his drive, he voiced a one-word expletive. The nun warned him about the wrath of the Lord. As the skies darkened, the priest skulled his fairway shot into a sandtrap. The priest's expletive was answered by a bolt of lightning. The nun fell dead. The priest fell dumb. From the angry heavens came the voice of the Lord: "*Merde!*"

Karen's pale hands flew to her mouth to muffle laughter. "*Merci.* It's such a long way from the street to the cloister. You bring back Bay Ridge. Our Flatbush house had no windows from which to look out and see my sweaty brother shouting words that awaken streets and life. *Mon frère,* who was blamed for every broken window on Fortieth Street." She paused for breath. "I have questions. I must have the truth to take with me. And, please, break the stained-glass window between us."

Knowing his agony was yet to be, Devers said nothing.

"Why didn't you or father join the church with mother and me?"

There was a time to be silent, a time to speak. The time for silence had gone with their lives. "You needed a miracle. Pop and I didn't."

Karen said nothing about her rheumatic heart. "What miracle did mother need?"

"Your faith in miracles."

"Did she share my faith?"

Devers shook his head.

Karen prayed for her mother before she confronted her brother. "Aren't we all in need of miracles? Wasn't Frank Merriwell a miracle you needed?"

"A miracle or a god?"

"Same thing," said Karen. "Wasn't Emrich Vanbroeck a miracle father needed? Wasn't father forsaken when that gaunt old man wedded to his money died in—what year was it?"

"March 11, 1933."

"Of course. Vanbroeck forsook not only father, but also you."

"I still had Frank Merriwell."

"Yes, 1933. I remember December of that year. I also remember father forsaking you. Why did he?"

Devers chose to lie. "Because I left him and ran off to college."

"That was 1936. In December of 1933 I heard father refer to you as *that Jew bastard.* Why?"

Devers told Karen an unfunny story: father stealing out of the house late in the afternoon, opening both pairs of garage doors but not securing them against the wind, sitting in the Buick, warming up the engine and going nowhere because he had no place to go; he watching from his bedroom window, seeing the wind slamming the garage doors shut, running out to open and secure the garage doors and returning upstairs without saying a word.

Karen prayed for her father. "Did mother ever know?"

"I told her that night. When Pop took his after-dinner walk to Church Avenue. We made decisions. To sell the house and set Pop and me up in business."

"You were at Erasmus."

"I graduated in February."

"Oh, God, the hours father and you put in."

Devers said nothing.

Karen said, "I was so happy when mother wrote me that you were going to South Carolina. So bewildered when you dropped out at the close of your sophomore year. You were so happy there. Why, Dev, why?"

He did not tell her all the truth, only that South Carolina was not Princeton, and that the offer of a sportswriting job in Greensboro was too good to turn down. Moreover, Mag was graduating.

"You ran from Margaret. Why?"

"You're wrong."

"Margaret believes you ran from her."

Devers gave Karen a secret to take to her grave. "I ran from Mag's mother."

Karen failed to understand at once. He told her just enough for understanding. She commiserated with him until she posed the next question.

"I remember 1936 as a bad year for us. Where did the money to send you to South Carolina come from?"

"Jacob Wald. Mom's father."

"His estate? He died in 1915."

"He died in 1940."

Karen winced. "Did *ma mère* lie to me?"

"In 1915, when Mom married Pop, Jacob Wald rent his clothes and mourned her as dead. In 1936—for my sake—Mom went to see him. For the first time since 1908."

She was confused. "These dates, these years. 1908?"

"The year Mom entered Barnard. Against Jacob Wald's orders. He didn't believe in education for women. Mom left his house and went to live with Aunt Minnie."

"Oh, God, if I could sit and talk to you for a year!" She grasped his hands. "Questions, questions. *Mon frère,* what are you going through?"

"I'm the well one," he said.

She shook her head. "I look into your eyes and I see the winter eyes that cry for the wind to blow garage doors shut."

Devers tried to smile. He failed to speak.

"Simone Weil said the Holy Grail belonged to him who asked the wounded king: 'What are you going through?' Answer me, please."

He tried. "The boy hiding within me won't let me accept

the death of things." She was listening. "I think I may have to kill him before—"

"The boy's dead. Since 1933. Slain by Emrich Vanbroeck."

"No," said Devers. "He's alive."

"When was the last time you ran in your sleep?"

"It's been years now. Before Dallas."

"Isn't that proof enough? The boy who runs for Princeton in the geography of his dreams has departed from you."

He told Karen how the boy still waked the dead. In the geography of his current dreams, Jack Kennedy was in the White House, the *World-Telegram* on the newsstands, Miles and Donna at home, and a girl with cornsilk hair in his bed.

"*Askesis,*" said Karen. "The dark night of the soul."

Devers thought it was a good name for a horse and said he would check the racing forms. He was *the well one.* He had to be. Big race today, big wedding reception tomorrow.

"You're not invited," he said.

"I'll be there," Karen vowed.

"Everybody'll be there. Pop, Mom, Mr. Vanbroeck, Jake the bootlegger—"

"Jacob Wald? Was he a bootlegger? Mother said he was a butcher."

"Butcher, bootlegger, inventor of calendars, worshiper of numbers. He prayed to God that he might wake up one morning and understand Einstein. So he begat a daughter who begat a son who begat a son who understands Einstein. Isn't that what Mom meant when she talked about sweet America?"

"Yes. Oh, yes." Karen dried tears before she spoke again. "Some years ago, the father of one of our novices told me how delighted he was to have learned that I was your sister. When he said you were *a good sportswriter,* I committed the sin of *hubris* and told him that you had won a Pulitzer Prize for a series of *religious articles.* He said he remembered those columns as vehement protests against the Brooklyn Dodgers and the New York Giants moving to Los Angeles and to San Francisco respectively. I didn't relent. I instructed the gentleman to read those articles again—in your book—and to regard them as jeremiads against the destruction of temples. Lastly, I impressed upon him the truth that Ebbets Field was as sacred to you as St. Peter's in Rome is to me."

Devers thought Karen was wrong, the gentleman right. He thought about the ball park still standing for the boy hiding within him. He wondered how large a wrecking ball it would take to destroy the boy.

"It shouldn't be," he said. "It won't be, once the boy in me is gone."

Karen was distressed, but she was diverted by the entrance of Sister Alicia. The visit was over. The doctor was on his way.

Devers did not stir. He faced Karen. "A last question?"

"Is there an answer to a question I may have forgotten to ask?"

"Shall I tell you what Pop told me before he died?"

"Please."

"He said the warmest place in the world was the valley between Mom's breasts."

Tearful, trembling, Karen embraced her brother and, for the first and last time in their lives, she kissed him on the mouth, as their mother had done to him before she died.

Karen said she would pray for Donna. She asked him to give his daughter the light in his eyes. At the very least, the light he had the night Donna was born. At the very most, the light he had before Vanbroeck forsook him.

Devers was on his feet when the doctor entered. He was at the door, unable to leave, unable to shut it. He wanted to keep the door open for Karen as he had kept the garage doors open for his father.

"Dev!" Karen's alarm matched his own.

He turned to her.

"Beware of the boy," she whispered.

FIVE

It was almost one o'clock before Devers parked the Thunderbird around the corner from the entrance to the apartment house where Charlie Spencer had nothing more than an address. He rang the bell three times before he went for the key Charlie had entrusted to him. Before he opened the door, he saw Charlie dead. In the disarray of the modest apartment he saw the obscenity of life.

The living room stank of dead cigars. The floor was a riot of hundreds of typescript pages, a splintered bottle of drugstore bourbon, a pair of shattered eyeglasses, and fragmented plates of false teeth.

In the bedroom Devers smelled whiskey, perfume, and cigarette smoke before he saw the paunchy figure of Charlie Spencer clad in boxer shorts and undershirt. The face was masked by lace-trimmed panties.

Behind time's mask, Devers saw the Dartmouth halfback, the sportswriter for *The Evening Telegram,* the *World-Telegram,* and the *World Journal Tribune,* the Scripps-Howard war correspondent.

He saw Charlie in Debden, he saw the change from big shot to big drunk to big brother. Charlie dubbed him Mister Memory and sold him to the *World-Telegram.*

Charlie and Francine were family. Charlie was his best friend and remained his best friend after the crisis of 1951: Devers passed Charlie on his way up. But Charlie had character, grace. Devers was his find, his friend, and he defended him and his success. He promoted the Pulitzer Prize for him.

And then the deaths. One after another. Francine. The *World Journal Tribune*. Devers tried, Mag tried, Charlie himself tried, but nobody could put Charlie together again.

Devers raised the blinds and the windows. Unmasked, Charlie opened his hollow eyes, managed a toothless grin, and ran a hand through his hairless head. He complained of a Hungarian whore sitting on his head and blamed her for stealing his teeth.

In a familiar bureau drawer Devers found a spare pair of eyeglasses and a set of dentures. His sight and bite sure again, Charlie identified Devers as the guy from Campbell's funeral parlor.

When Devers mentioned the Belmont Stakes, Charlie could not have cared less. He refused an Alka-Seltzer and ordered a bloody mary with two Swedish meatballs in it.

Still in bed, Charlie was drinking alone, sounding off about the lousy job of editing sports books for boys that tried to paint Babe Ruth as a Jesus with a baseball bat, losing his temper, and chasing Devers to Belmont.

Devers told him the news about Donna and Herbert Mouritzen. To Charlie it was good news, bad reporting. He wondered if Devers had read the item on the *Times* obituary page.

When Devers revealed the bridegroom's age, Charlie told him to go fuck himself, all the three-year-olds at Belmont, Toots Shor, and all the sportswriters who didn't think thirty-seven was young, who did not know that Donna was as smart as she was beautiful.

Devers accepted the retort as called-for and correct. Charlie was right and he had to do right by him. He returned the subject to horses. It was a place to begin, a place to save both of them. Belmont Stakes, a possible triple crown for Forward Pass. Charlie should not miss it.

Charlie was deaf to Devers until he left the bed, made it to the kitchen and the bottle of drugstore vodka. He listened to the vodka pouring into his glass, to his pleasure in drinking it like water, before he confronted Devers.

Which Forward Pass mattered? The horse running at Belmont or the boy who runs in his sleep for Princeton? Another question. What was Charlie Spencer's big day in football?

Devers recited an answer: the afternoon Charlie scored a touchdown for Dartmouth against Yale in Yale Bowl.

Charlie corrected him. It was a night in New Orleans, in the Roosevelt Hotel, when he tackled a Princeton end named Forrest Devers, who was running from his bed, in his sleep, toward a ninth-story window. Charlie chided himself. He should have missed the tackle. Had he done so, he would not have missed being in Toots Shor's last night and being syndicated in eighty-six newspapers.

Devers had Charlie where he wanted him now, and it was time to put the question to him. Before he spoke, he changed his tack. He implored Charlie to write the Sunday column for him. He gave his reasons: the wedding reception, Karen, his sleepless night, his black mood.

Charlie was not buying it. He would go to Campbell's before he went to Belmont.

Deep in his despair, Devers found an out for himself, an in for Charlie. He suggested that Charlie cover the race from his apartment. On television. Channel 2, at five o'clock. There would be thousands at Belmont, but millions in front of television sets. Moreover, there was a horse named T.V. Commercial in the race.

Charlie said nothing. His demeanor said nothing. He left the kitchen and Devers did not follow him. He recognized preoccupation.

It took five minutes for Charlie to return to the kitchen and to Devers. With the same preoccupation. Devers said nothing. Charlie said it all.

It had been a strange year. The Masters decided by a pencil, the Derby by a needle. What if Forward Pass won and they paid off on him? What if, on Monday, the Nielsen report came out and gave the race to T.V. Commercial?

Devers allowed Charlie all of the enthusiasm. He told Charlie to write the column in the form of a letter, as Charlie had done on other occasions in the past. When Charlie nodded absently, Devers said something about delivering a case of Wild Turkey to him on Sunday night.

The preoccupation was gone, the understanding was there.

Charlie said, "Tell Mag not to worry. I love Donna enough to stay away."

"You be there. I ordered a case of Canada Dry ginger ale."

"I'll be in Hartford."

The meaning of Hartford was clear to Devers, but he did not relent. "Donna'll be in Valley Stream. Stay on the wagon, Charlie. From this minute to the minute you leave Donna laughing."

"Fuck you, sergeant!" He flung Devers back to Debden. "Get the hell to Belmont! I don't want to be your guest columnist! I don't want to be your guest tomorrow! And I don't want to be your friend on Monday!"

"What about Tuesday?"

"Don't patronize me."

"Drysdale's pitching. Thought we'd fly out to the coast and—"

"Fuck Drysdale. I hold the shutout record. Three hundred and ninety-five days."

"I can count, too."

"Beautifully. Up to eighty-six."

Devers chose not to play on words, not to lure Charlie with eighty-six beautiful newspapers. "The hell with the column. Forget it. The hell with the reception, too. Just help me to exorcise my *dybbuk*."

Charlie was intrigued. "Then what?"

"Let the *dybbuk* possess you."

"What if I say no to you?"

"Then I'll have to kill the *dybbuk*. Before it kills me."

Charlie paled. "How do you kill a *dybbuk?*"

Recalling what Jacob Wald had told him about kosher slaughtering, Devers said, "With a perfect knife, and an untrembling hand. The *dybbuk* must be parted from me with the ease of a strand of hair drawn out of a pitcher of hot milk."

Charlie drew near to understanding. "This *dybbuk*—has it got a name?"

"Frank Merriwell."

Charlie's eyes opened wide enough for Devers to see the light cast by two black candles.

SIX

The feeling that he was late plagued Devers as he crossed from the garage to the front door. He was about to put the key in the lock when he saw the doorknob turn. He prepared himself for the gray hair, the dark stare, and the black mass.

A wisp of a girl with honey hair, almond eyes, and a raspberry mouth favored him with a stratosphere smile.

"Hi! I'm Letty Hines!"

The friendly skies confused him.

"You don't remember me."

He studied the girl in the Malibu skimmer. "I'll never forget you again."

"I moved away when I was fourteen."

"And how old are you now?"

"Twenty-two. I was always two years older than Donna and always looked two years younger. Isn't it simply marvelous about Donna?"

Devers agreed, excused himself, and went to the master bedroom to learn how marvelous it was with Mag.

Mag was composed but tense as she sat at her desk holding the telephone, smoking a Salem, and sipping black coffee. She gave him a harried glance, concluded the call, and voiced her complaints. "My sisters are in Atlanta for the weekend and, of course, they can't possibly make it. Donna's plane is due in at 6:40 but it probably won't be able to land for an hour or more. And I've been on the phone all day and I hardly have a voice left."

"Do we have a *minion?*" He noted the hazy, hurt look. "Will we have a crowd here tomorrow?"

"I didn't plan on having a *crowd here tomorrow.* Only a proper—"

"Anyway, it was smart of you to round up a stewardess."

"Letty? Donna invited her. Hasn't she grown up nicely? She'll be sleeping in Donna's room, Donna and Herbert in your den, it being so separate and private, and I don't believe they'd mind at all, do you?"

"It'll be a little crowded, the three of us in—"

"You're sleeping here tonight."

"Who's been booked into Miles' room?"

A flare of anguish. "Is it too much to ask you to sleep where you belong for just one night? Must you shame me before Herbert?"

"No. Anything you want me to do?"

"I've done everything. I've managed quite well without you."

"I'm proud of you," he said. "And I'm sorry about your sisters."

"I told Donna she should have told us well in advance what she was up to."

"Was it a pleasant call?"

"I'm her mother and I have to remind her of that. But I was very pleasant to Herbert and he was so very pleasant to me. He has such a good voice and such a good choice of words. And so mature."

"I'm glad," he said, crossing to the door.

A brusque question stopped him. "Did you talk to Charlie?"

"Charlie will arrive and leave on the wagon."

"He'd better."

Devers said nothing about Karen. He left Mag and Staten Island for the smile of things in the living room.

"When did you see Donna last?"

"Oh, a year ago last spring in Los Angeles. We've been writing to each other—regularly—ever since we moved to Omaha. Donna writes such wonderful letters. She's *so* smart. You're all *so* smart, and Miles—well, he's a genius."

"Do you like Miles?"

"Heavens, did I have a crush on him! But, of course, he never noticed me. How could he? I was so young, so awfully skinny, and so giggly."

"You're only two years younger than Miles."

"I told you. When I was fourteen, I looked like Twiggy, only it wasn't cute and popular to look like that when I was fourteen."

"By the way, have you heard anything about dinner plans for tonight?"

"Yes, sir, we're going Chinese. I made the reservation for Mrs. Devers on your telephone. The Canton House."

"Good. I'll trade fortune cookies with you."

She expressed a delight which in another hour would make him hungry for more. "Would you? You used to do that with Donna. She told me. Whenever your fortune was better than hers, you'd trade with her."

"I'll do the same for you," he vowed.

"Oh, I like you. And, oh, that picture of you and President Kennedy!"

He did not wish to think of Arlington.

"Let's see what's in the Frigidaire. There's one thing about a Chinese meal, you find you're hungry an hour before you have it."

"You mean *after,* don't you?"

"You're so right."

"What did you and President Kennedy used to talk about?"

"Girls."

She laughed. "You're silly. Donna says you write the silliest letters. She just loves them."

"How often do you write home?"

"I telephone home every couple of weeks or so unless I get the blues."

"You have a large family, don't you?"

"Yes, sir. Three brothers and three sisters. And mother's still skinnier than I am. I've been accused of being frigid."

"American Airlines propaganda."

Letty was carrying on about the burden of her virginity when Devers put her to work. "Stewardess, may I have a Wild Turkey on the rocks?"

"Coming right up, sir."

Devers was alone for an instant before he heard Mag calling him.

Coming right up, sir, coming right down, Mag. Ceiling zero, all wild turkeys grounded. No boys in the White House talking about girls. Big girls, little girls, lace panties on the tennis court and long legs and longer drives on the golf course. Daughters and funny faces.

Requiescat in pace, dear Jack.

SEVEN

The doorbell rang at 7:25 P.M., Eastern Daylight Savings Time. Devers saw an Italian boy, a Detroit truck, a small beribboned box, a long beribboned box, but not the color of twilight. He answered the question about his name, signed a receipt, slipped a dollar bill into the fine Italian hand, and shut the door upon the emptiness rioting through the winding street.

Deciding not to disturb the ribbons or his curiosity, he deposited the two boxes on the hall table. He was en route to the bottle, and to a soft chair, when he heard the door to his daughter's room burst open.

Letty Hines danced out in her silken minidress and sang out the coming of the bride and groom. She was out the door before Devers came to it. He saw the taxi and to the right of it he saw Donna and Letty embracing. In another instant he had eyes only for his daughter, for the long, straight raven hair, for the blue eyes, and for the apparition of his mother as a girl.

When he turned and looked the other way, Devers saw

Herbert Mouritzen: very tall, lean, cold, thinning blond hair, rumpled seersucker suit, buttoned-down white shirt, blue bow tie.

He saw no more because his daughter's face was rushing toward him. The sun and the moon were through the clouds and she was upon him, in the universe of his arms. She kissed his cheek and he kissed her cheek close to the mouth belonging to the man carrying two valises.

While Letty gaggled away, Donna introduced her husband to her father, and Devers gave his son-in-law the smile he had given to Jack Kennedy. Herbert responded with a quantum of a smile.

As the girls rushed in the direction of Mag's outcry which knew no doors, Devers took Donna's valise from Herbert and led the way out of the house, into the breezeway, and to the den.

Devers inquired about the flight, the airport, the taxi problem, and Herbert allowed that he would detail his complaints in a strong letter to the mayor. When Devers tried a jest about Harvard complaining to Yale, Herbert made it quite plain that he considered himself a Wisconsin man.

Certain he was a Tanqueray man, Devers served him a perfect drink. Herbert, who saw everything and said nothing, thanked him and made no comment about the drink, the den, the photograph, or the prize. He did ask for consent to use the telephone.

Having given it, Devers tore himself away. He got as far as the bar in the living room, where he stood and listened to the sound of one bedroom wing flapping. Far above all others, Mag's voice prevailed. Soon Letty Hines appeared. The stars in her eyes died when she drew close enough to whisper to Devers.

And he listened and said nothing as she understood that brains were more important than looks in a man but she never knew that Miles had such old friends who were old in years and she did think that Devers looked younger than Herbert and she couldn't believe what she saw when she saw Herbert and no wonder Donna didn't tell her much about Herbert on the telephone but brains are more important than looks or anything although she wondered and worried about marrying a man who looked like Herbert and the truth was there were so many men in the friendly skies of United who were handsome and come to think of it at the friendly bar of Devers there was a handsome man who looked younger than Herbert with whom she couldn't think of getting in bed and my God was there something really wrong with her after all because—

To shut up her whispers, Devers took her from the living room down to the rumpus room to shoot a game of pool. She was carrying on about how she believed every good American home should have a room with a bar, a pool table, an upright piano, a color TV, a stereo, room for dancing, and a dart board, when he broke the rack.

She inquired what game they were playing and what they were playing for. He did not tell her that every time he sunk a ball she would have to remove an article of clothing, and that every time she sunk a ball she would be allowed to sink one of her hands into one of his trouser pockets. He did tell her, as she leaned over to make a massé shot, that she did more for pocket billiards than Willie Hoppe had ever done. He was explaining that Willie Hoppe was the Cantonese genius who had invented almond duck when he heard the voice of turmoil.

It was Mag and she was soon down the stairs and into her cross-examination: what was the number of his drink and what was Letty drinking and did he know that the flowers were from Charlie and that the roses for Donna and the orchid for her were very nice but did Charlie have to say something stupid on Donna's card like from the one you jilted.

Mag then turned to Letty and told her to go upstairs and take her orchid. Alone with Devers, Mag issued the orders of the day: no more drinks here and just one drink at the restaurant and, please, no dirty stories, and remember not to offer to drive because she was driving because she wouldn't want her daughter and her son-in-law killed in a traffic accident.

When the newlyweds appeared in the living room, Mag was her old self, and an old, good warmth returned to the house. All went well, even the ride to the Canton House. Mag made it by staying in the right-hand lanes and by fooling the Evil Eye into believing the station wagon was part of a funeral procession.

Devers made one jest in the restaurant: had there been six of them, they would've gotten Ho Chi Minh. The man from the think factory did not think to laugh. He was too busy putting the menu through a computer.

Nevertheless, Herbert proved he could use chopsticks and that he could eat and criticize the food at the same time. And, of course, the only superb Chinese food was to be gotten in Paris in a Left Bank hole-in-the-wall run by two Indo-Chinese chefs.

Herbert drank his Tanqueray gin, but did not smoke, did not swear, did not tell off-color tales, and was Wyatt Earp when it came to drawing his Dunhill lighter whenever Mag drew a cigarette to her nervous mouth. And Herbert held the floor, the table, and the fascination of all but Devers, who learned more than he wished to know about Southern California, marinas, sailboats, and the superiority of foreign sports cars.

Devers did trade fortune cookies with Letty. His had read: *Be expecting happiness in a letter from somebody far away.* Hers had read: *Don't be thrown off balance by a muddled friend.*

EIGHT

Mag, Donna, and Letty had stolen away to the master bedroom for girl talk. Down in the rumpus room, across the bar from Herbert, who nursed his brands of gin, silence, and discomfort, Devers drank Old Bushmills with no pleasure.

Uncorked spirits flowed easier than talk between two unlike spirits. Devers knew that Herbert had no interest in the deflation of football at Harvard, the caging of Willie Mays inside the wire fence around the Candlestick Park outfield, the shaming of Joe DiMaggio in white baseball shoes in Oakland, or the laughing at the Shea Stadium comedy act of Mets and Jets.

He knew enough to avoid mention of Miles, or of his own occupation and preoccupations. And he did not give a damn about Herbert's views on politics, war, friendship, and kinship.

One game at a time, as Charlie Spencer always said when he mistook a bar for a press box. The game was marriage, the game between Herbert and Donna. All Devers hungered for was one answer to one question. Why had Herbert taken Donna as his wife?

He thought it wise to get Herbert to talk about Herbert.

"What are you doing at Rand?"

"That's classified," said Herbert.

Devers said nothing. He never made the joke about disappointing his superiors in Moscow.

Herbert surprised him by saying more. Rand was where Miles belonged. Not *Ramparts.*

Devers had a thousand questions. He asked none, for he knew the field was mined.

Herbert went on. He immediately involved Devers by saying that Frank Merriwell could no longer win wars for America. Devers did not retort that beating Hanoi was like the old New York Yankees beating a Sally League ball club during spring training.

Herbert was wound up now. He believed America should make a nuclear show of force against Hanoi, if need be. First he favored trying chemical warfare. Chemical and disease weapons. Botulinus toxin, for example. One ounce of which, theoretically, could destroy sixty million people.

Devers had a question about the thousands of sheep out West killed last March.

An accident, according to Herbert, caused by the release of nerve gases. He went on to describe the terrible deaths suffered by the sheep. Sick unto death, Devers took more Irish whiskey. Its taste was gone, its medicine spent.

As a physicist, Herbert declared he was not committed to biological and chemical weapons. He was involved with the possibilities of an extremely powerful beam of carbon dioxide gas laser. In peace it represented a breakthrough in communications. In war, it might be the harbinger of the death ray.

Devers listened. Herbert was as wild as Rex Barney and he was warming him up in the bullpen.

Death rays were not comic book inventions. Life is not comic. Life is war. Life wars on life. Herbert alluded to the dinner at the Chinese restaurant. To nourish Devers' life and his, eggs were stolen from hens, hens were slaughtered, as were a pig, a duck, a steer, shrimps, and lobsters. Flesh demands flesh, life demands life.

Devers poured more gin into Herbert's glass. One ice cube, one cold question. Where does man go from here?

The future, said Herbert, would, perhaps, take man to the cattle pens. He foresaw a possible invasion from another planet, a takeover of the earth by a form of life far in advance of earthmen. These conquerers would herd billions of people, the prime and favored source of meat.

When Devers asked if this was a possibility or a probability, Herbert was quick to respond. A possibility. A probability was a Communist invasion. The Prince of Peace had come and gone. Hegel, who praised war, remained with us.

Devers said, "You were just married. When you think of a wife, children, and a home, don't you dream of peace?"

Herbert hesitated. "Yes. And I dream of the work I'd rather be doing. Exploring the skies. Looking for a link with a possible supercivilization within the Milky Way."

He went on to explain he would be working, as a physicist, with radio astronomers and mathematicians, his task involving experiments using laser beams as a mode for signaling distant worlds.

Herbert kept talking. About Gauss and Pythagoras and schemes to make contact with Martians, about Siberia and a right-angled triangle large enough to be visible on Mars, and about Martians perhaps knowing that the square of the hypotenuse of a right triangle was equal in area to the sum of the squares of the other two sides.

Devers kept listening. He remembered having heard about this scheme from Miles, and having understood it better than he did now. These things did not stay with him. The thing he understood now was that Herbert was almost at ease.

Devers waited. For a time he was lost in space with biochemistry, symbolic logic, and cosmic language. At the proper moment, when Herbert poured more gin into his glass, Devers tried to bring him down to the moon.

"What about the moon shot? Does it interest you?"

"It annoys me. I deplore the Frank Merriwell aspect. The Russians did it with Gagarin, the Americans with Glenn. It's not the man in the rocket, it's the men who put the rocket on the moon. It's science."

Devers skirted the Merriwell issue. "It's a great story. The first man on the moon. A greater story than Lindbergh or Columbus."

Herbert disagreed. Lindbergh did not build his monoplane, Columbus his ship. Neither invented the compass, the sail, the internal combustion engine, or the rudder. Moreover, he preferred, for space travel, programed robots rather than daring Merriwells.

Devers asked, "Do you have or did you ever have any heroes you worshiped?"

"I worship nothing. I frown on heroes. I frown on Miles playing hero at *Ramparts.*"

"Is that what he's doing?"

"I think he thinks so. I don't. I see him taking money from the National Science Foundation with his right hand, and from the enemies of America with his left hand."

"What enemies of America?" Devers saw the enemy before him.

Herbert sighed. "Oh, let's not get into politics."

"You're into treason."

Herbert met his stare but said nothing.

"Get yourself out of it, Herbert."

"Miles is twenty-four. I'm thirty-seven."

"I'm fifty-one."

"I can't talk to him anymore. Can you?"

"I listen to him. Do you?"

"Donna tells me you're not happy about Miles and *Ramparts.*"

"That's politics. Not treason."

"They can be one and the same thing."

"How could you marry the sister of a traitor? What will they say down at Rand? At the FBI? At the Pentagon? Will they trust you anymore to produce your nuclear show over Hanoi?"

Herbert emptied his glass and rose. "Good night."

"You're not worried?"

"Not at all. The schism between Miles and me is common gossip in the math and physics departments at Harvard."

"Is there a schism between Donna and you?"

"No. And there never will be."

"Why did you choose Donna?"

"I love her."

"You're not a college kid. You thought long and hard about it. Why, at long last, Donna?"

Herbert looked away, for an exit. He faced Devers before he turned in another direction to receive a signal from a distant planet, from a super-intelligence. He was not addressing Devers when he spoke from a region halfway between his mind and his heart.

"Why Donna? Because I believe that she, above all others, will never commit treason against me."

Devers felt as sick as the sheep who fell victim to the escaping nerve gas. He checked his agony and muted his outcry. "What kind of treason?"

His eyes on the pool table, Herbert hesitated before he spoke. "The kind—"

"Look at me!"

Herbert obeyed. "The supreme treason would be for Donna to let me down when I needed her most."

A perfect answer to an imperfect question. And not a damned moment too soon. For into the rumpus room flew Letty and her flying mouth. The invasion of a not so super-intelligence from skies clouded with coffee, tea, or milk caused Herbert to climb to the upstairs altitude. Devers retreated as far as the radio for a signal of music.

"What kind of music is that?" asked Letty.

"Mozart. One of the three B's."

She did not get the music or the joke. She did get Devers. "You look so sad. What are you thinking?"

"Who was the boy who looked after the sheep at Yale?"

"What?"

"Frank Merriwell. You probably never met him. He flies the base paths. Clouds of dust trail him."

"I don't know what you're saying, but I like to hear you talk. You hardly said anything in the Chinese restaurant."

"An hour after you hear anything I say, you're hungry for more."

"Please. Who is Frank Merriwell?"

"The best of the best. He stood for every boy's dream. For truth, faith, justice, the triumph of right. He had nobility, he walked in armor."

Letty asked, "Where is he from?"

"A Dutch village beyond Sandy Hook, where God was a Dutchman. A Princeton man, who told Frank Merriwell that his heaven was not in New Haven but in New Jersey. Frank believed him and packed his dreams for Princeton. Then he was told that God was dead, and the Princeton dream died in the suitcase. And the ghost of the dream came out to haunt Frank and make him run in his sleep. For Princeton."

Devers took more Bushmills.

"It's like music," said Letty.

He sang McCormack.

"You sing better when you talk."

"So Frank Merriwell broke his baseball bat in two, made a crucifix, and planted it on the grave of his boyhood. And then he went to Russia, hit a home run over the walls of the Kremlin, and was sentenced to be shot at dawn. Princess Anastasia intervened with the Czar, and Frank Merriwell was sent down to Siberia. There he met a Greek by the name of Pythagoras, a very well-known underachiever, who suggested that they seek fame and fortune by manufacturing gigantic right-angle triangles, for which there was a great potential market on the planet Mars. But Frank Merriwell countered with a brilliant idea of his own. Together they would buy a baseball team, for he'd read in *Pravda* that the Vladivostok Russkies were for sale. The idea being to move the franchise across the Pacific to Brooklyn, and then to Boston, and then to Milwaukee, and then to Atlanta, and finally to march baseball through Georgia and into the sea. For what began in the sea with the fishes must end in the sea with all games postponed on account of the rain that fell for forty days and forty nights. All of which led to Noah's problem with the ark and taking only two of a kind, and when it came to picking two Irish kikes, God put forward the names of Walter O'Malley and Horace Stoneham. And God saw that it was good."

"It's Herbert, isn't it? I could tell in the restaurant."

"Life," said Devers, "is built into the chemistry of the universe. Just as gravy is built into boardinghouse steaks."

The next voice Devers heard was that of his wife calling from the light at the top of the stairs. "Dev!"

"Yes, Mag."

"What are you doing down there?"

He remembered the joke. We're fucking, Mother, replied the boy. That's nice, don't fight, children. He did say, "Bart Hodge locked me in."

"It's midnight," said Mag. "Donna and Herbert wish to say good night."

"Yes, Mag." He emptied his glass and turned to Letty. "Not a word about Herbert. We must be kind to visitors from far-off planets. They're not like you or me. They have no navels, and having no belly-buttons just sort of spoils the whole idea of a bikini, which I understand is having a problem with radioactive crabs."

Letty laughed. The girlish laughter meant nothing to Devers until the night locked him in with Mag.

Sunday, June 2, 1968

ONE

The dark tomb oppressed Devers. He wanted to tear down the drapes, smash the shutters, shatter the windows, touch the budding roses, and feel other thorns.

Mag was oppressing him. Lying close to him in bed, she was developing prints: bleak pictures of the future, dirty pictures of the present, and X-ray plates of the past that was mystery. There was no pattern to her musings, doubts, and questions.

He heard her and said nothing until she demanded to hear from him. He chose the evasions of tired quips and yawns, but he could not make it to silence, to sleep. She persisted. He endured.

Mag kept returning to Donna. In anger she reminded Devers of his own anger with his daughter in the recent past. She raised dust, threw mud, retreated to contrition and to avowals of loving and caring. She so much wanted Donna to be happy. She was not sure Donna looked happy. She wanted to know if Donna looked happy to Devers.

He considered the question, and he tried, for once, to make sense. He thought the question was wrong. The right question was this: did Donna look happy to Herbert?

Mag mistook this for wry humor. She was so far from understanding that Devers decided against telling her what

Herbert had told him about Donna, love, and treason. He did say he was sure Herbert was happy with Donna.

Devers' constant defense of Herbert dismayed Mag. She confessed she sometimes wished she had never met him. She had never noticed him on the campus. She was two years ahead of him, had no classes with him, and ran with a different crowd. She blamed her father for inviting Devers to live with the Griffins on Pendleton Street. But she stopped short of the reason and the panic behind her father's action.

She gave the reason another name. Miles. Her brother. If her brother Miles had not died, Devers would never have come into the house to take his room. And her heart.

She spoke of her love for her brother. He was like no one she had ever met. She wished she loved her son Miles the way she had loved her brother Miles. What's in a name? Her son was a stranger she had never known or understood. He brought her more pain than pleasure. He brought her Herbert.

Devers brought Mag to Staten Island. He told Mag about Karen, her condition, and her pleasure in receiving a telegram from Donna. He recited the message. It was a mistake.

Mag wore out five questions. Why did Donna ask Karen to pray for her? What is Donna afraid of? Is she afraid of Herbert? Is he too old for her? Is he wrong for her?

His patience worn away, Devers suggested Mag take a red one and let sleep answer her doubts. She countered by turning on him now. She went to the past for questions half a lifetime of sleep had failed to answer.

He refused to listen. Leaving the bed, he went to the bathroom. In an instant Mag was behind him, warning him not to take a single seconal. She reminded him that he had been drinking, and that Dorothy Kilgallen had been drinking before she took the sleeping capsules that killed her.

Devers took two aspirin. Mag took one seconal. She counted

the capsules remaining in the plastic bottle. Eighteen. She told Devers she expected to find the same number in the morning.

Sleep was long in coming for Mag. It came by way of lamentation. The gray in her hair, the lard on her body, the empty nest, the husband so far away in his hideaway.

And then, near to sleep, Mag was roused by a strange side effect of the drug: insight.

As she searched the past, she found questions too close to secrets caged in Devers' mind. He had released secrets to Karen because she was close to death. Mag was not. And, even if she were, he felt he would bury the unsaid in his own unanswering grave. He had to. The answers would drive her up the wall and out of her mind.

To shut her up, he drew Mag into his arms. She was responsive, she was desperate when she failed to rouse him. The past was upon Devers, in the touch and feel and desperation, in the closet feeling of the dark. And he was impotent until the boy hiding within him conjured Letty Hines. Deaf to Mag's sweet cry, he took Letty Hines before the boy hiding within him could change her into the girl sleeping in his hideaway bed.

Mag wept. Devers listened to the good weeping. Mag slept. One red capsule. One red-faced lie of love.

Facing the ceiling, the roof, and the night sky beyond, Devers raised his arms and reached for stars.

Lord have mercy, a honeymoon cottage for two, but never two in a tomb. Love has no chance in a tomb dark with time, death, and guilt. Lord have mercy.

Devers heard the boy within him cry out for the destruction of the tomb. The cry died away and Devers listened to a silence singing sweeter than McCormack.

TWO

Devers saw that Letty had no interest in the menu or in the little girls having a slumber-party breakfast at the big table. He was about to tell her that he could not see Donna or her among them when he saw the death of things bearing the weight of the Sunday *Times.*

Mel Teller. Friend, neighbor, family physician. Older and shorter, paunchy and balding. He caught Devers' smile, and brought a frown to Letty. "Are you the new son-in-law?"

Devers laughed. Letty said, "You know me, doctor. I'm Letty Hines."

Teller sat down, the frown persisting. "You had such a nice name like 'Herbert Mouritzen.' Why'd you change it?"

She said, "It was—you don't remember—but it was nine years ago—on a Sunday morning as a matter of fact—that my dad brought me over to your house after he'd hit me in the eye with a baseball."

Teller frowned. "You're *that* Letty Hines!"

Letty laughed and shook her head. "The two of you! What a pair!"

"I told you people will talk. Dev, we can't go on like this anymore."

Devers said, "What used to be, used to be, is no more."

Teller nodded. "That's one song you never heard McCormack do. Even when his name was Richard Tucker."

He turned to Letty and examined her eyes. "And what team is your father pitching for now?"

"It was nine years ago and—"

Teller held Letty's hand. "I want to save you." He looked askance at Devers. "From *him.* Look at him. You see what happens when you have a Gaelic father instead of a Galician father?" He turned from laughter to bewilderment. "Letty, you're beautiful enough for both of us. Stop laughing before I give you such a black eye. Such a hit. Such a face." He kissed her hand. "Will you run away with me today?"

She nodded. "After the party."

"After you run away with me, *then* we'll have the party. I'm only inviting you and me."

Letty said, "I think I'd like to be married to a doctor."

Now Teller regarded Devers with disdain. "Did you hear? Did you see? And you said Bermuda shorts were unbecoming to me."

The waitress appeared and Teller did not joke with her except to order a cup of cream with coffee on the side.

He turned again to Letty. "How are you?"

"I'm fine now, doctor."

"And how are your folks?"

"Just fine."

"Then how come they skipped town without paying me their last bill?"

"You mean that?"

"The only patients I remember are those who don't pay their last bills."

She was concerned. "How much was it?"

"Sure, you run up a bill with a poor, struggling doctor, you fly away, and you don't have the slightest idea of how me and my family are suffering. Do you know that my wife is driving last year's Cadillac?"

Letty said, "I never know when you're serious or not."

The food was served, and the talk that followed concerned the horses at Belmont, the primary in California, the wedding reception, and life in the stratosphere.

When Letty left the table to join a boy and a girl with whom she had gone to grammar school, Devers lit a cigarette and observed Teller. "Mel, what's wrong?"

"What should be wrong? Give me one of your cigarettes."

Devers played dumb. He knew that his friend had been a three-pack-a-day smoker until another doctor had ordered him to desist or die.

Slapping a penny down on the table, Teller said, "Here's a penny. Sell me a cigarette."

"Sorry. No Sunday selling."

"Do you want me to have to get up from this table and walk over and buy a whole pack of —?"

"What is it, Mel?"

"No Sunday talking. It's party time. Soon."

"Talk," Devers urged him.

Teller turned away and glanced at Letty. "You know what's wrong with this country? If a girl isn't an American beauty—like Letty, like your Donna—she doesn't belong. She has no place, no life. She opens a magazine, turns on the TV, goes to the movies, looks at the newspaper ads, and then makes the mistake of looking in the mirror. And then of stepping on the scales. Did you and I have bathroom scales when we were kids in Brooklyn? To weigh yourself, you needed a penny. And did we think of reducing? We thought of eating, of fixing ourselves so we wouldn't die of pneumonia or consumption." He turned to Devers. "Anyway, look at me. Do I look like a scared kid?" Devers said nothing. "Do you know what it means to be fifty-five and to be a scared kid?"

Devers asked, "Who, what, when, where, and why?"

Teller took a deep breath. "A girl named Nancy Glaviano. Nineteen. My patient. Problem: obesity. And it's my problem because her folks are old patients of mine and they believe in me like I was Jesus Christ. Two months ago Nancy made the first try. Twenty-five seconals. My prescription. But she didn't die. Because, like I do with all of my patients, I mix half and half. Half of the capsules were placebos. Well, I called in the best psychiatrist I know. You met him at my house. Joe Fischer. Good man." He paused to crack knuckles. "Thursday. Five-thirty in the morning. I get a telephone call from Mrs. Glaviano. Mr. Glaviano and his sons are in Washington Market. Mrs. Glaviano's alone. Nancy isn't in her bed. Nancy isn't in the house. Please, God, please, Jesus, would I rush over? I rushed. Red lights and all. For God's sake, Dev, give me a cigarette."

Devers gave him a cigarette.

"I got to the house. I gave Mrs. Glaviano a sedation. And then I went where I had to go, where I feared to go. I've been a doctor for almost thirty years. I've lived with death. But going down those stairs to the dark basement I was a kid again. A kid scared of crapping in his pants." He drew at the cigarette. "Behind the boiler. Above an old stool she'd kicked away. Hanging. Her mother used to tell her and keep telling her that she had such a nice face, a very nice face. It wasn't true anymore. It was ugly. God, it was ugly. God, it was frightening. God, I was a kid crying for my own mother to take me away, to make me over, and not to make me into a doctor who's not a doctor when he has to walk alone into a dark basement and—"

Teller shut up. Letty was back. He stood and then sat down beside her. The tears still in his eyes, he regarded her as his long-lost love. "You came back." He took her hand and kissed it. "I knew you would." He glared at Devers. "He said you wouldn't. He doesn't know you. He doesn't understand you. You're not flighty, are you?"

Letty, perturbed by the tears, said, "No—"

"No, you're Letty Hines. Soon to be Mrs. Melvin Teller."

"Look, I'm sorry if—"

"We're in this together. You drove me to it."

She turned to Devers for help.

Teller frowned. "Forget him. His name is Forrest. And what is a Forrest by any other name? A forest is a *wald.* Letty, my love, let me take you away from this *finsterwald,* from this *schwarzwald.*"

Letty told Devers she was going with her old friends to see their apartment before she found a smile for Teller. "I'll see you later, doctor."

He said, "I'm glad I found you out. You're fickle. You're cheap. The least you can do is pick up the check."

"I haven't a cent on me."

"I love you." She moved away. Turning to Devers, he said, "She lied. She has a scent. How would you describe that scent?"

"Sunday morning in June."

"I'll remember that."

"Remember to forget the basement."

"What do you prescribe, Dr. Devers?"

"Pears and wine."

Teller killed the cigarette. "One of Nancy's thighs was as big around as Letty's waist. And her brain was big enough to tell her to double the clothesline rope."

"Pears and wine," Devers repeated.

"You'll forgive me if I forget to dance at your daughter's wedding."

"First drink, then dance."

A smile. "I'm all right now." He took the check and signed it. "I just remembered. I was going to call you later this morning. Something very urgent. A pitcher named Rixey. What's his first name? Four letters."

"Eppa," said Devers before he spelled it.

"You'll make Ruthie very happy."

"Haven't I always?"

Teller said, "I must talk to Joe Fischer about you and Ruthie. Must be some kind of code in those crossword puzzles. And doesn't it suggest something when my tootsie only has trouble with four-letter words?"

"Like Helfelfinger?"

"I remember that. And I remember you telling me that was German for Merriwell."

They were in the parking lot, outside of the doctor's Continental Mark III, when Teller said, "Pears and wine?"

"Yeah."

"And what are you going to have?"

"A party."

"Don't kid me. I saw you with little Letty, and you didn't look like you were with lovely Letty. You looked like you were down in the basement with Nancy Glaviano."

"E-p-p-a."

"Is that German for death?"

"Pears and wine."

Teller got behind the wheel and started the engine. "Thank you, Dr. Helfelfinger."

Teller drove away. Devers looked for his Thunderbird until he found it on Staten Island. He drove the station wagon home by way of Nancy Glaviano's basement.

THREE

Devers saw his 1966 Plymouth coupe at the curb and rushed inside to remove the apron from Mag's party dress now worn by Lola Dowtin. He was reminding her that today she was a guest when Mag intervened to inform him to call Operator Six in Cleveland.

And Devers understood that the truth of the morning was blacker than Lola Dowtin.

It was by way of Charlie Spencer's apartment that he went to the den. He had spoken to two operators, one secretary, and was waiting to hear outrage tempered by Hun, Wharton, and Wall Street when he saw Fortieth Street, Dewey Junior High School, Manual Training High School, Hotchkiss, Yale, the Marines, the Philadelphia Eagles, and Fallon's Steak House in Bay Ridge. Six-two, two-sixty-five, Jack Fallon, born of an Irish father and a Bavarian mother, looked like a German general in mufti.

Devers managed a smile and kept Fallon from withdrawing.

He was about to explain the nature of the call when he heard Curtis Buchanan's voice.

"Forrest?"

"Yes, Curtis. How are you?"

"Disturbed."

"I'm sorry to hear that."

"I enjoyed your column this morning. As a matter of fact,

I enjoyed it immensely." Devers said nothing. "Immensely. Until I read a name that spoiled my Sunday kippers."

"Charlie Spencer," said Devers without apology.

"Let us refer to him as *him.*"

"*Him* wrote the column." The apparent lapse of grammar caused Fallon to look up from *Life.*

"And who requested *him* to do so?"

"I did, Curtis."

"Might I inquire why, Forrest?"

"I needed help."

"Are you ill?"

"As you are this morning, so was I yesterday."

"I beg your pardon."

"I was disturbed yesterday."

"By what, Forrest?"

"I became a father of the bride."

"Congratulations."

"Thank you."

"It won't happen again, will it?"

"I only have one daughter."

"Then I take it we understand each other."

"No, Curtis."

"You know my feelings about *him.*"

"You're a big man, Curtis. You can forgive and forget."

"Not where it concerns *him.*"

"Curtis?"

"Yes, Forrest?"

"How about if I have *him* write you a letter of apology?"

"I have no wish to hear from *him.*"

"You might like what you read."

"I remember vividly what I read in the *Times.*"

"He was drunk. He was heartsick. His wife died in March. His newspaper died in May. It was too much for one man to—"

"It was never *his* newspaper."

"The newspaper was his life, Curtis."

"What about my life, Forrest?"

"You're still in the newspaper game."

"I also have three sisters, two daughters, and two sons. All of whom are versed in the style of English printed in *The New York Times*."

"You can make Xerox copies of his letter of apology and distribute them to all interested parties."

"And then what?"

"And then you can put *him* back on the payroll."

"Forrest, it is impossible for me to conceive of contributing to his burial fund."

"Just think of putting *him* back on the payroll."

"In what capacity?"

"He's the best sportswriter in the country."

"Excluding Red Smith, Jim Murray, you, and—"

"Including me."

"Let the *Times* hire him."

"The *Times* has Daley and Lipsyte."

"Lipsyte is younger than Daley. *He* is not younger than you."

"Read the column again, Curtis."

"And you, Forrest, are much younger than Daley. Is it getting too much for you to write five columns a week?"

"Yes, Curtis."

"And what new arrangement do you suggest?"

"Three by me, three by *him*. At no additional expense to you."

"I might be interested." Devers did not bite. "Provided, of course, you can possibly make the arrangement with someone other than *him*."

"Have you anybody in mind, Curtis?"

"I might suggest two names."

"I'm listening."

Buchanan mentioned two young sportswriters. Devers was not interested.

"Forrest, I have another suggestion."

"I'm listening."

"Miles Devers."

"He won't listen."

"To you or to me?"

"To either of us."

"Surely you don't approve of what Miles is doing now, do you?"

"What's un-American about mathematics?"

"I was referring to *Ramparts*."

"What's un-American about *Ramparts?*"

"Put it to Miles. You have nothing to lose."

"I can lose Miles."

"How do you mean?"

Devers decided against telling Buchanan Miles' opinion of the Scripps-Howard newspapers. He said, "Miles brooks no parental suggestions."

"I'm sorry. Somehow I was led to believe that you and he were very close. I envied you that."

"Miles passed me a long time ago."

"Miles wouldn't be the first young man to outgrow radicalism."

"Don't bet on it, Curtis."

"Where shall I place my wager?"

"I made *my* suggestion."

"Forrest, I'll be candid with you. Before I did that, I'd return to investment banking."

"It's your life."

"Do we understand each other about *him?*"

"No, Curtis."

"I don't like your tone."

"And I don't like yours. I was never in Wall Street but thanks to Scripps-Howard I've got fuck-you money."

"Goodbye, Mr. Devers. Mr. Alderholt will be in touch with you."

In Cleveland a click, in Valley Stream Devers poured bourbon for Fallon and himself before he explained what had happened.

"Jesus, I'm sorry."

"Jack, have we got a party?"

"You've got the fixings."

"Where are the eggs?"

Fallon heard the imitation of his own boyhood voice and fought tears. "What are you going to do, Dev?"

"Today?"

"Tomorrow."

"Yesterday I drove by Fortieth Street. Looked all over for you. Didn't see you running out for a pass and knocking down a horse."

Fallon downed his drink. "You didn't see anybody eating an orange—skin and all. Or a banana—skin and all. You didn't see anybody using a rusty razor blade for a toothpick. Or anybody sewing up a gash in his hand with black thread."

"Hey, Bull, let's blow up that Davega football. You blow it up. I tie the bladder. You hold the bladder down. I lace it. You throw it, I catch it. Touchdown, Fortieth Street."

Fallon said, "Jesus, you make me either want to laugh or want to cry."

"How's business?"

"Judy and I were talking in bed last night."

"I like Judy."

"I love her. But I don't like her. Sometimes. It's all right to be tiny in size, but it ain't right being small."

Devers wanted to tell Fallon how small Curtis Buchanan

was. He said, "Judy's human and, as Noah could tell you, that ain't a very large animal."

"My wife's small. My mother was a big woman and she was small. My mother didn't like your mother and your father. Or you. She was kind to your sister because she was such a sick kid. But it bothered her because your mother and father went to college, because you were the smartest kid on the block, the smartest—"

"You just heard how dumb I am."

Fallon ignored him. "Not the same with Judy. Sure, she's a Manhattanville girl, and I'm a Yale man, but she can't forgive you and Mag for having such bright kids. Miles waltzed into Harvard. My boy Gary couldn't make it into any Ivy League school. Nothing wrong with Ohio State, but try telling that to Judy."

"Jack, do me a favor."

"What?"

"Don't apologize to me for Judy."

"I have to. I have to keep telling her from time to time how it all was. And how it would've been if it hadn't been for you."

"Why the hell don't you remember you're Fallon of Yale and shut up about Fortieth Street?"

Fallon was not quiet for long. "Why'd you drive by the old block yesterday?"

"I was on my way back from Staten Island."

"How is Karen?"

"The sick one is sick." He changed the subject. "Judy and the gang with you?"

"Just Judy and Gary are coming, and they'll be along. You know Judy. She'd die before she'd be the first one to arrive at a party."

"Where was Judy going today?"

"To her folks in Jersey."

"Have a spat?"

"No, I learned from you. I gave her the silent treatment until we got in bed."

"Then you snored."

"No, I talked about Fortieth Street."

Devers said, "Bull, without me, you could've eaten up all those twelve-egg omelets all by yourself."

"They were good, weren't they?"

"They tasted the best when you found the eggs in the laundry bag. Wrapped up in one of your mother's corsets."

Fallon laughed. "Jesus, yeah. Those were the days."

"This is one of those days. We're having a party."

The familiar complaint. "We don't get together like we used to. I sure miss those St. Patrick's Day parties."

"You didn't forget the Swedish meatballs, did you?"

"No meatballs."

"You won't forget my son-in-law."

"Judy doesn't like him because he's Harvard."

Devers said, "At least Judy doesn't hide the eggs."

"I gave up on eggs. Cholesterol."

"How about oranges and bananas?"

"I peel them."

"Like cutting Samson's hair."

"When are you going to get gray or bald?"

"I'm Lefty of the Little League."

"I never got a real kick out of playing Princeton. And you know why."

From the Vanbroeck mausoleum in Greenwood Cemetery Devers said, "I don't like running guards who run off at the mouth."

"What are you going to do tomorrow?"

"Shake hands with O'Malley and play first base for the Brooklyns. Did you know there's a Brooklyn Avenue in Los Angeles?"

"I was listening, Dev. When you talk, I listen. You know that. What did you mean when you said, 'I could lose Miles'?"

"Buchanan's stupid enough to think Miles might be interested in his money. Devers & Son, sports columnists."

"Beats Sixtieth Street, don't it?"

Devers smelled sawdust. "Bull, do you remember Sixtieth Street and Devers & Son?"

"I don't like what I remember."

"What do you remember?"

"Jesus," said Fallon, "it was an ass-freezing place. I remember that first Christmas I came back from New Haven. I remember walking in on you when you were glazing a pile of sash. I remember the look on your face before you saw me. You didn't smile or laugh until you saw me, and you were all smiles and laughs when you took me to lunch at Pete the Greek's place. But I remember the look on your face before you saw me. I saw it again when you were on the phone with your boss."

Devers said, "Look for the eggs. That's the secret of life. The egg came before the omelet."

"That's why I was trying to tell Judy the—"

"Jack, shut up about Judy. This is Donna's day."

"Dev, we don't get to see each other—"

"We came to your birthday party."

"Almost three months ago." Fallon was bluer than the sky over Yale Bowl. "It's not like it used to be. We don't get to talk, you and me."

"We're a quartet," said Devers. "We're supposed to sing."

"Who's a quartet?"

"Judy, Mag, you, and me."

"No, we're not. And I miss you. I need you to pump me up the way you needed me to pump up that old Davega football."

And Devers pumped him up with the golden past and the golden eggs before Fallon was able to bounce out of the den.

Alone, Devers found he did not miss Fallon. He missed what Fallon missed: his column in the *World-Telegram* and, for a time, in the *World Journal Tribune.* He did not miss the meaning of Curtis Buchanan's curt farewell: Goodbye, Mr. Devers.

FOUR

Devers went back before Dallas to recapture the party feeling: the fun and games, the corned beeves and cabbages, the Irish whiskeys and wines, and the corny programs prized by his guests.

The program cover was the art of Willard Mullin, the *World-Telegram* sports cartoonist. Page two was devoted to a burlesque history of St. Patrick's Day, brought up to date each year with fresh evidence discovered in the Dead Sea scrolls. Page three was given to a floor plan of the house and a map of the grounds for "the poor sheep lost with strange wives." Pages four, five, and six listed the fun and games, more for fantasy, less for the fancy free. Pages seven through eleven contained the Scouting Report. Scotch-taped to the back page was an envelope holding two aspirin tablets, one Kleenex, and the business cards of a divorce lawyer and a psychiatrist.

At 1:46 P.M., at a time when Devers was wondering if the Verrazano Bridge had fallen down, the first guest arrived.

Charlie Spencer. And nobody clapped hands but Charlie.

He was drunk. With joy. Joy was driving up to Hartford at dawn, buying the *Courant,* and reading the column he had written for Devers.

Devers conjured the 1963 Scouting Report:

"CHARLIE SPENCER . . . *World-Telegram* sports staff . . . store-bought teeth give him a bite worse than his bark . . . scored on Yale, the Everleigh Sisters, Polly Adler, and Madame Butterfly . . . Dartmouth '29."

You're a good man, Charlie Spencer. You're a bad man, Curtis Buchanan. Ginger ale for Charlie. Bitter herbs for Curtis.

As were their habits, the early ones came early, the late ones late. The complainers voiced guilt for having been forced to make this a Sunday of disappointment for parents, in-laws, children, grandchildren, neighbors, business associates, and one mistress around the corner from Park Avenue.

They came with less hair, longer hair, longer sideburns, heavier jowls, increased fat, hollow laughter, empty eyes, mounting ailments, and further reports on the dying and the dead.

Ruthie and Mel Teller.

She (". . . plays doctor when the doctor is out of sight . . . Ziegfeld, 36–24–36 . . .") missed Devers' familiar pat on her girdle. He (". . . the doctor is IN like Flynn . . . makes house calls in the bushes . . . NYU and Bellevue, where he was also a mental patient . . .") came up from Nancy Glaviano's basement.

Maxine and Hal Groves.

She (". . . a flower of the Old South who demands constant deflowering . . . Agnes Scott '42 . . .") greeted Mag with a warmth reserved for sisters of her sorority and her South. He (". . . public relations, sexual relations . . . known to grounded English lasses as the Beast of Debden . . . Duke

'38 . . .") received a salute from the staff sergeant who had served under him in the 4th Fighter Group's public relations office.

Carla and Sanford Wald.

They were family, but they were never invited to any of the St. Patrick's Day parties. She was a rabbi's daughter, he a first cousin to Devers, a son of his mother's brother, a Manhattan orthodontist. They were not a fun couple, now or ever.

Joanne and Roy Hadley.

She (". . . fools around with the theater . . . and with anyone who happens to be in it . . . Boston University '47 . . .") came in sporting the latest color from Clairol. He (". . . *World-Telegram* sports desk . . . also can do it in a chair . . . Holy Cross '41 . . .") entered with the Sunday afternoon news from NBC Sports.

Trudy and Dom Caruso.

She (". . . not Italian, except in bed with another Italian, who need not be born Italian . . . Earl Carroll 37–25–36 . . .") entered wearing armor from Lane Bryant. He (". . . covers the Mets for the *World-Telegram* . . . covers Trudy on the late late show . . . St. John's '46 . . .") made straight for his boss, Hal Groves.

There was equal billing and unequal kidding of friends and relatives: the cousin's husband who was "an executive with the Brooklyn Union Gas Company, makers of knishes and stuffed derma," the stockbroker neighbor whose first wife was "alive and well in General Motors, IBM, and Boeing," the South Carolina alumna who was "a redheaded reason why the South lost the war and won the boudoirs," the judge who "believes in capital punishment, whips, chains, and strong bedposts." And so on.

And then, at last, came the Mouritzens.

They had to wait until noon before they were allowed to

visit Karen. They brought black bulletins. Bad night. Sedation. A detailed report later. In the den. From Donna to Devers. One on one.

Devers bided his time, played host and clown, and held up the Brooklyn side of the Verrazano Bridge on his stressed shoulders.

And the doorbell rang. Forsaking the remembrance of silly things past, Devers put together names and faces.

Elsa and Marvin Ragovin, the latter his mother's sister's son and a Macy's salesman; Florence and Seymour Rosenfeld, the latter the science editor for *Newspaper Enterprise Association;* Marcia and Sid Patrick, he of the Associated Press sports staff; Bess and Joe Hyman, he of the *New York Post* sports staff; Pam and Lloyd Rowland, he of *The New York Times Magazine;* and Izzy Title, once an accompanist to Al Jolson, also to Ring Lardner, Rube Goldberg and Grantland Rice.

And then came the members of the Now Generation, friends, relatives, and neighbors, each sharing the secret knowledge that time and life had begun with them and would end with them.

The doorbell never stopped ringing: telegrams, the wedding cake, Judy and Gary Fallon.

There was a party, thanks to Jack Fallon and his team of bartenders, waiters, and cooks. There was a party and Devers was there.

He heard Herbert Mouritzen say to Seymour Rosenfeld: "Historically physics employed mathematics dealing with continuous quantities, such as calculus and derivative fields. Now I find more interest in the probability theory and in the math of discrete, noncontinuous phenomena of the sort best handled by linear algebraic methods. . . ."

Florence Rosenfeld said to Devers: "Did you know that Seymour and I have willed our bodies to the Columbia Medical School?"

And he looked at her and he could find no wit and no words. He excused himself to inspect the scene: the flow of spirits, the course of the cigarette smoke, the laughter of the Now People, the laments of the Then People.

In other rooms, he heard other voices.

Said Charlie Spencer: "I never knew how beautiful Hartford could be on a Sunday morning."

Said Izzy Title: "You ought to get your piano tuned. Things were better when sportswriters lived on the North Shore."

Said Carla Wald: "Sanford's going in next week for a prostate operation. He doesn't think I know, but I know it's malignant."

Said Herbert Mouritzen to Seymour Rosenfeld: "The prospect is hell on earth. When scientists and politicians act out of ignorance and pretend it's knowledge, they're putting the world in extreme hazard."

Said Mag: "Dev, I hope you're not drinking too much."

Said Judy Fallon: "He looks forty-five to me."

Said Hal Groves: "Dev, it's been one helluva year. Business couldn't be better. But, damn it, it's Debden all over again. We've lost six men since Christmas when Burt Gilmore put the gun to his head. They're shooting us down like flies."

Said Letty Hines: "It's a real fun party!"

Said Gary Fallon to Letty Hines: "You're supposed to drink ginger ale the day *after* the party."

Said the same Herbert Mouritzen to the same Seymour Rosenfeld: "It has taken Homo sapiens, thinking man, half a million years to reach our present population figure. And Homo sapiens, unthinking man, will double it in thirty years or less. Unless he begins to think and to act."

Said Florence Rosenfeld: "Dev darling, you haven't commented."

Said darling Dev: "You'll both be a riot at Columbia. They'll probably hold you over."

Said a bartender: "Yes, sir, Mr. Devers. Wild Turkey it is."

Said Joanne Hadley: "You can't possibly understand Pinter unless you understand the language of the dead silences between the dialogues."

Said Mag: "I don't want any crap game on the pool table."

Said the very same Herbert Mouritzen to the very same Seymour Rosenfeld: "I believe our concern is to conserve the human spirit not from the hell hereafter—but from hell on earth."

Said Devers to Mel Teller: "No, it was Dave Bancroft who played shortstop for the Giants before Travis Jackson."

Said Ruthie Teller: "Herbert and Seymour seem to be having a nice honeymoon."

Said Lloyd Rowland: "Your boy Miles, he did quite a piece for us on Reagan. Sure like to steal him away from *Ramparts*."

Said Devers to Fallon: "Where are the eggs?"

Fallon laughed. "You know what you're going to be saying from now on? Where's the bill? And there's not going to be any bill."

Devers understood him and understood the futility of a debate before an audience of a smoked Vermont turkey, a Smithfield ham, and a baron of prime beef. "Yeah, but what about my money-back guarantee?"

Leaving Fallon laughing, Devers followed the rock music blowing in his ear from the rumpus room.

There was no crap game to break up. Izzy Title, at the silent piano, was sitting the wrong way on the bench. The other crapshooters, including Charlie Spencer and Mel Teller, were sitting the wrong way on the bar stools.

The crapshooters were girl-watchers, and their eyes were

dying stars light-years away from the beautiful and the beheld.

The party was young, the sky was dark, and thunder announced showers that threatened to rain on Forrest Devers' parade.

FIVE

The knives were at the turkey, the ham, and the beef. The Now Generation took over the tables on the back lawn, leaving the rumpus room to Izzy Title and the piano, to Mel Teller and the voice unlike Tucker's or Jolson's, and to Charlie Spencer, who wondered aloud to Forrest Devers what kind of song Curtis Buchanan was singing in Cleveland. Devers lied more beautifully than any of the beautiful songs by Berlin, Kern, Gershwin, Youmans, Rodgers, Donaldson, and Henderson.

And then Mrs. Herbert Mouritzen came downstairs to blow in her father's ear, receive his nod, and depart. While the singers were advancing on Berlin, Devers retreated. He took time and care to compliment Jack Fallon. He noted that Herbert Mouritzen was still talking to Seymour Rosenfeld, but this time he made no attempt to overhear him. Instead he stole away to the den beyond the breezeway to hear what his daughter had to say.

He entered to find Donna seated at the desk, brushing her fingers over the Remington keys, but making no sound, no music. He was a boy in a woodshed until she spoke and changed him into her father.

"How many times have you had this old thing reconditioned?"

He sat close to the desk and felt old. "I've lost count."

"I never could use it."

"You broke it once."

"How old was I?"

"About ten."

"What was I writing?"

He did not remember, and he brought additional pain to the pain of forgetting. "A note telling me you were running away from home."

"I don't remember that." She kissed her forefinger and ran it across the keys before she faced her father again. "Wasn't I writing a love letter to Junior Caldwell?"

He remembered that Second Lieutenant Philip Caldwell, Jr., had been killed in a strategic hamlet north of Saigon. He said, "When you were ten, Junior was sixteen and playing quarterback for Valley Stream High."

"I remember the way you used to throw the football with Junior. And with Miles."

He ran to San Francisco. "What did Miles say on the phone?"

"He threw the football."

"No kicks?"

"My brother has a good coach."

"I try."

"Yes, you do. It was a lovely party."

"Is it over?"

"We'd like a taxi." She glanced at her wristwatch. "In half an hour."

"Yes, Mrs. Mouritzen." Devers, who knew the number well, had to consult his Blue Book. The call was made, the taxi ordered. "Where are you staying in Washington?"

"The Carlton."

"Nice hotel."

"So Herbert tells me."

The clocks were running, the taxis were running. "What did Herbert tell you to make you Mrs. Herbert Mouritzen?"

"It's not what he told me. It's what he *asked* me."

He misunderstood. "I wasn't suggesting you did the proposing."

"No, of course not."

"When did he first ask you to marry him?"

"Last Sunday night."

"When did you accept his proposal?"

"Last Sunday night."

"No hesitation on your part?"

"No, Dad."

"Any hesitation on Herbert's part?"

"Considerable." She smiled. "There were questions I had to answer."

"Such as?"

She hesitated. "I do owe you candor, don't I?"

He was lost. "You owe me nothing."

"I believe I want to tell you. I wanted to tell Karen. I would have, had I been alone."

Karen was dying, he was dying. "What did you want to tell Karen?"

"About *the* question."

"Only one. You said there were questions—"

"*One* question. *The* question. The others had meaning, and I had no trouble answering them. Honestly, I might add."

He tensed. "How else but *honestly?*"

Her smile did not wait for the taxi. It fled. "There's deception."

He made light of the dark. "Poppa don't allow no deception in here."

"There's always deception."

"It's no sin to be deceived."

She hesitated again. "*I* was the deceiver. Pay close attention. Concentrate. The worst has happened. You happen to be a survivor, but not for long. The earth is contaminated. Now you find yourself on a pebbled beach where you see another living human being. An old man. In one hand he holds a black velvet bag. In the other hand one white pebble, one black pebble. He offers you one chance to survive. A game of chance. He will drop the white and the black pebble into the bag. Should you reach in the sack and draw out the black pebble, you'll be left to die. Should you, however, draw out the white pebble, the old man will give you the secret of survival. Of course, you agree. But then you spy the old man dropping *two black pebbles* into the velvet bag. Now what do you do?"

He asked, "How much time do I have?"

She studied two black hands. "Twenty-four minutes."

"Donna, how long did it take you to answer it?"

She was candid. "I couldn't answer it. I couldn't have answered it in a million years."

He was confused. "Is that how you answered Herbert?"

Her voice died. "No. He asked me the question at one o'clock in the morning. And then he left me. I called him two hours later. With the answer. He proposed. On the phone."

With no mind to bring to the riddle, he relented. "What's the answer?"

"Aren't you going to try, Dad?"

"I've lived a million years."

"This is the solution: you put a hand into the bag, take one pebble, and withdraw your hand quickly and nervously so that the pebble seems to slip from your grasp. So that the pebble falls to the pebbled beach. Then you face the old man and tell him to draw the remaining pebble from the bag. For, if the pebble in the bag is black, then you must have drawn the white one."

"Who gave *you* the answer?"

She cracked her knuckles, a habit for which, when she was only thirteen, he had given her ten dollars to break. "One guess."

"Miles."

"Yes, Dad."

He remembered not to scold but to reach into the velvet bag and bring out a jewel of empathy. "Did you tell Miles that the question had been put to you by Herbert?"

"No," she said with contrition.

"How long did it take Miles to come up with the answer?"

"He asked me to repeat the problem. As soon as I mentioned the pebbled beach, he stopped me and said, 'I've got it.'"

"And Miles just rattled off the answer?"

"No. He directed me to it."

"How?"

"Miles told me not to think of the stone to be removed from the bag. But to concentrate on the stone left in the bag—and on the place of the meeting." She smiled. "I did. And I came up with the answer. I thanked my brother, hung up, and immediately called Herbert." The smile was lost now. "It was only after I'd agreed to become Mrs. Herbert Mouritzen that I realized the—the deception."

Devers said nothing. His mind was on the stone left in his heart.

"Dad, do you understand me?"

"No."

"I so much wanted to be Mrs. Herbert Mouritzen that I accepted—that I led myself to believe I'd only accepted a hint from Miles. That the answer was mine. I believed the answer was mine because I wanted to believe it."

He was thinking of how many black lies could be contained in a velvet bag. "Have you told Herbert this?"

"No. He knows how much I love him. I had to tell you—because you didn't know."

"Don't you think Herbert knows you telephoned Miles before you telephoned him?"

"He asked me to marry him."

"It was three o'clock in the morning."

"We were married in the afternoon. Of the following Friday."

Devers did not relent. "What would've happened had you called Herbert at three in the morning and told him you didn't have the answer?"

"We'll never know, will we?"

He flung the stone that put her conscience to flight. "We'll never forget, will we?"

She fought him. "Shall I tell you what I do know?"

"I wish you would."

"I have the answer. Herbert's the answer."

"Yeah. But what was the question?"

"Who is Donna?"

"Who *is* she?"

"Don't you know?"

"I don't know how Mrs. Herbert Mouritzen looks back on Donna Devers. Tell me."

"I was Forrest Devers' daughter. And then I was Miles Devers' sister."

"Nothing more?"

"Dad, what more was there?"

He remembered Karen and her plaint about not being able to talk to him for a year, and he pretended the taxi was a year away. "Shall we begin at the conception?"

"If we do, I'll be asking the cab driver questions only you can answer."

"You were in such a hurry to be born. For a time I thought the damn cop was going to have to deliver you in a 1948 Chevrolet."

She repeated the question. "Dad, what more was there?"

"Six pounds, eleven ounces. Wearing a bracelet spelling out—"

"Dad, please."

"Would you like a diamond necklace for a wedding gift?"

"You can afford more."

"You name it."

"I'd like understanding. Your special understanding."

"You have it."

"I'm afraid of losing it in the taxi."

"Shall we wrap it up in a black velvet bag?"

"I want it in my heart."

"About Forrest Devers' daughter. How did he go wrong with her?"

"You didn't go wrong. You only had me wrong."

"Would you explain, please."

"Donna Devers was a pseudonym for the reincarnation of Miriam Wald."

"Are you dropping out of UCLA?"

"No. Herbert wants me to graduate."

"Good for Herbert."

"Dad, let's, for a moment, leave Herbert out of this. This is between you and me. And Miles."

"Let's leave Miles out of this."

"We can't."

"Can't we try?"

"When I needed an answer, I called Miles at three in the morning. When you needed an answer, you called Miles."

"Your mother told you."

"Yes. And obviously you didn't tell mother everything Miles told you."

"No, I didn't. Miles is wrong about Herbert."

"Is he, Dad?" Her voice was choked.

"If he's not wrong, then you are."

"Honestly now, Dad, don't you, deep down, feel that you're wrong and Miles is right?"

"Donna, who said you weren't bright?"

"I did."

"Beginning when?"

"Beginning with awareness."

"And when did that begin?"

"With voices. Your voice. Miles' voice. And all of those dialogues between you. Beginning with baseball and football. Ending with God and gods."

"Were you listening?"

"No, I was listening for the telephone to ring."

"Always?"

"I listened to Mom. She compared. But you, Dad, you were never guilty of that. You never compared me to Miles."

He said, "I can't compare myself to Miles. Fatbelly, you remember Miles. You remember more than you should. Try now to remember the day when baseball and football died with God and gods. When Miles stopped asking me questions. When Miles began to speak a language spoken by Herbert Mouritzen and Seymour Rosenfeld."

"I understand, Dad. I'm not complaining. I'm only trying to explain myself."

"Forgive me, I thought I detected resentment."

"I never resented you. I never resented Miles."

"Herbert isn't a father image, is he?"

"Do you resent that?"

"Probably. Is there such a thing as a brother image?"

"For me there is," she said. "The image isn't physical. It's—it's intellectual." She shook her head. "There must be a better word."

"Do intellectuals bring babies into the world?"

"I expect my graduation gown to hide the fact of my pregnancy."

He went forward in time with her. "What happens if the baby is a boy who eats up all twenty-six volumes of the Britannica and then comes to the dinner table to discuss Pythagoras with his old man?"

Donna looked hurt. "Old man?"

"Freud or no Freud, I didn't mean it that way."

She believed him. "When that happens, I'll smile on the outside and cry on the inside. Because—and I hope you understand this, Dad—that's the dream I've settled for."

"Does the dream remain a dream if you only *settle* for it?"

She glowered at him. "Dad, don't do it. You're doing something ugly now—something very unlike you."

"What am I doing?"

"You're chewing on my words and you're spitting them back at me. What's wrong with *settling* for a dream? And why shouldn't the dream remain a dream? Am I asking for a miracle to make me an actress like Katharine Hepburn. I chose UCLA for its Theater Arts program, and I found out what I had to. Well, that dream isn't a dream anymore." The tears came. "I know who I am. I'm no Hepburn, no Miles, no Miriam Wald. I'm no longer Donna Devers, no longer on the telephone. Believe me, Dad, I'm bright. I'm Mrs. Herbert Mouritzen and my husband's not too old to give me sons like himself. Or Miles."

He had nowhere to go but to humor. "What if your boys turn out like *your* old man?"

"That can't happen," she said, attending to her tears.

"No, I guess not."

"I'd like it to happen."

He heard her and he loved life and her again. "Thanks. I'll have the *dybbuk* warm up on the sidelines."

"What, Dad?"

The taxi was coming, the parting was coming, followed by the sorrows and the silences. He said, "When your boys are boys, look for me in them. And, when they approach manhood, hide them from me."

Devers was following his daughter's sad eyes to the sadder photograph of two smiling boys in the White House when into the room burst a drunk and hysterical girl. Letty Hines.

SIX

The party was over.

Mag was spent. She had no questions, no wish to chat, nowhere to go but sleep.

Devers checked the doors, the lights, and the ghosts in the dark before he went to the den to rouse Letty Hines and return her to Donna's bed.

The lamplight failed to wake her. John McCormack failed. Devers succeeded with a touch.

Letty had a question about the hour. It was seven minutes before ten o'clock.

She had shame and she spoke of it, of how Gary Fallon had shamed her into drinking champagne and of how he had made a pass at her in the garden.

Interested only in ridding himself of Letty, Devers helped her to rise. She complained of dizziness and refused to leave the sofa. When he offered to summon Dr. Teller, she moaned and protested.

She did not like the doctor. He had put his hand under her dress. He had said she was the kind of girl he wanted to find alone in a basement.

Devers asked no questions. Letty asked him to still McCormack. He did.

And then mild hysteria. She had to go to the bathroom and she was afraid of standing up and falling down.

Devers assisted her. Warning her not to lock the bathroom door, he let her enter alone.

In a few minutes he heard her moan. She was afraid to stand up, she was afraid of fainting. He entered to find her trembling and perspiring. At once he wet a towel and cooled her before he carried her out.

They were in the breezeway before Letty's hysteria returned. She pleaded not to be taken to Donna's room before Devers returned her to the sofa in the den. For a little while.

He soon wished he had not relented. He was bored with her and her suspicions of Mel Teller and Gary Fallon. He was angry with her and her forebodings about Donna and Herbert.

The Wild Turkey helped. John McCormack helped. But still he heard her, and she was now talking about Forrest Devers.

She liked him. And she went on and on until he told her to shut up before he fucked her.

He had meant to scare her, to chase her, or to sicken her, but she was not sickened until he had fucked her.

And then he carried her to the bathroom, positioned her on her knees and held her hand as she surrendered champagne and caviar and pâté de foie gras and ginger ale and shrimps and lobster and smoked turkey and the whole fucking party.

As he washed her, she raved about dying and about God forcing open a door and plucking her from a pressurized cabin into a jetstream where she would float down and away to death and eternal damnation.

He did not interrupt her when she began to pray or when she began to vomit again. He preferred her vomiting to her praying.

Letty vomited for the last time when Devers told her she was going to spend the night in Donna's bed.

He went alone to the telephone before he led Letty to his daughter's bedroom, to her belongings.

Under the stars, Devers held Letty's valise, supported her body, and prayed that the hinges of his own mind would hold fast before her ravings.

The taxi came. When it was gone with the weeping girl, Devers turned toward the house and unhinged his mind. In the window of Donna's darkened bedroom he saw the ghost of his mother-in-law.

SEVEN

The door swinging into his sleep, Devers opened his heavy eyes and saw his mother-in-law. A burst of overhead light, a slamming door, and he saw Mag.

Naked to the sockets of her eyes, she danced from switch to switch gathering witnesses of light before she broke the stereo arm and smashed two McCormack records. Then, wheeling on her husband, she pitched the secret of her fist.

Devers caught a small bottle. No seconals, no placebos, but

no peace. He was thinking of Nancy Glaviano and of Miles' mathematics of probability when he faced Mag and sensed her certainty of impending death. She was feeling hell's heat and bleeding sweat.

Trying for the aplomb of a pitchman, he asked, "All out?"

She pulled at the roots of her gray hair. "I want you to watch me die."

"Suicide?"

"You murdered me!"

The scream took him from the bed to a window that he slid shut. Turning to Mag again, he was careful to betray no alarm. "Did you leave a note to that effect?"

Louder and clearer. "You murdered me!"

"Shall I unmurder you?"

"Watch me die!"

"Shall I call Mel over and have him watch, too?"

"No!"

"Would you like to talk to Donna before you die?"

The sweat poured. "No!"

"Miles?"

"No!"

"Your sisters?"

"No!"

"When did I decide to murder you?"

"I heard you! The two of you whispering in Donna's room! I saw the two of you from Donna's window!"

"You missed the vomiting."

"I know what I missed in the den!"

He tried to deny the truth as Letty herself had denied it. "I didn't sleep with her."

"I know you did!"

He decided to save her by sickening her. "What dress do you want to be buried in?"

"Shut up!"

"The Rosenfelds have willed their bodies to the Columbia Medical School. Would you care to do the same?"

He did not shut up. Because she was immune to his absurdity, he began with the absurd. And then he slipped into the graphic, the pornographic, the revolting, the disgusting, the nauseating. She seemed beyond it all until she rushed to the bathroom, sank to her knees, and emitted nothing but dry groans.

Devers, behind her now, forced two fingers of his right hand into her mouth. Her teeth snapped at the fingers. Despite the pain, he forced the fingers deeper. At the moment she began to choke, he withdrew his fingers and held her head as she succeeded in vomiting. Once and no more.

He flushed the toilet, and he did not wait long before he returned his bloody and bleeding fingers to her mouth, voiced an obscenity, and forced her to bring up more of sleep and the death beyond sleep.

While Mag remained on her knees, Devers filled a glass with water, added table salt, stirred it, and brought it to her.

"Drink this," he said gently.

She drank until the taste got to her. "What did you give me?"

"Potassium nitrate. Poison. You'll be dead in a minute and it won't be my fingers in your mouth—"

"Mother!"

Devers did not stir. He let fear hold Mag's head as she repeatedly surrendered the seconals, the placebos, and the lovely party.

He began to nurse her. He told her by his actions that he wanted her to live. After he had washed her, he took her up and carried her to his bed. She pulled the blanket over her head before he made the circuit of the switches and returned the room to darkness.

He sat upon the bed. No reaction from Mag. He drew the

blanket, uncovered her head, and saw that she was deep in sleep. Perhaps too deeply.

He went to the desk, trained lamplight on the telephone, and ignored his bleeding fingers as he dialed Mel Teller's number.

"Hello."

"Ruthie. Dev. Put Mel on."

"He's asleep."

"Wake him, please."

"What's wrong?"

"Wake him, Ruthie."

"Hold on."

"Thanks."

He heard the doctor. "Yes, Dev?"

"Mel, grab your black bag and get right the hell over here."

"Coronary?"

"I'll time you, Mel."

He did not time him. By the time he opened the front door, he saw the robed and bagged doctor. Devers shut the door and opened Teller's eyes with the empty pill bottle.

"Eighteen," said Devers. "Should make eight or nine placebos, shouldn't it?"

Teller asked, "Where is she?"

As they hurried to the den, Devers recounted the nightmare that was not a nightmare. Teller said nothing and Devers said nothing more as he observed Teller playing doctor with Mag: the cold eyes, the sure hands, the taut mouth.

Teller rose and turned to Devers. "Let's have a smoke."

Teller opened the door and went into the breezeway. Devers, cigarettes and matches in hand, followed him.

They were both smoking when Devers asked, "Hospital?"

"No."

"You sure?"

Teller was angry. "Who the hell's sure? The one sure thing about Nancy Glaviano is that she's dead. The funeral's tomorrow morning, and I've got to be there." He drew on his cigarette and exhaled. "I took *her* to the hospital. A mistake. Unless you've got to pump their stomachs, it's a mistake. The public shame makes the next try easier. Next time go by hearse." He studied Devers. "But I'm not sure."

Devers said, "Tell Ruthie I had indigestion, which I mistook for a coronary. She heard you say 'coronary.' "

"Sure. I better call her. She's liable to pop over any minute. When I left her, she was crying for you."

Teller telephoned his wife, told the lie, told her to go to bed, and finally ordered her to remain where she was.

When Teller returned to the breezeway, Devers asked, "Do you have to stick around?"

"She should be watched. Just in case."

"Can I do the watching?"

"Can you stay awake?"

"I don't have a funeral to go to tomorrow."

"Shit!"

"Anything you want me to do, Mel?"

"Take her pulse. Every hour. If it gets weak or too fast, wake me up."

"Thanks, Mel."

"Dev?"

"Yeah?" He was ready for the inquiry.

"Can I ask a question?"

"Yeah."

"Why?"

"Mag saw Letty kiss me before I put her in a cab. She thinks I laid Letty."

"Did you?"

"No, Mel," he lied.

"I saw the Fallon kid feeding her champagne."

"She was sick. I wanted you to look at her. She didn't want you to."

The doctor was forlorn. "I put my hand under her dress. It's still there."

"She puked it out."

"My hand?"

"The party."

"Wasn't St. Patrick's Day, was it?"

"No. But I tried."

"Watch Mag. She may try again."

Devers heard him, but he said nothing.

"Dev, I mean to scare you. You've got a basement, too. And isn't there a clothesline down there?"

"Yeah."

Teller returned to the den, killed his cigarette, and examined his patient again. Black bag in hand, he crossed to the breezeway and to Devers.

"Sure you can stay awake?"

"Damn sure."

"I'm going to crawl in bed with Ruthie. I'm scared shitless."

"I know. I'm scared, too."

"Question, Dev. Did you want to lay Letty like I wanted to lay her?"

"Yeah, Mel."

"I'm going to hold Ruthie and think about Letty because I don't want to think about Nancy Glaviano or Mag Devers." He looked hard at Devers. "Doctor's orders: *you* think about Nancy Glaviano and Mag Devers. Think about the basement and the clothesline and the hanging." His voice cracked. "Take the fucking thing down."

Not trusting his own voice, Devers merely nodded. He watched Dr. Melvin Teller leave for his wife's bed and for the hand under Letty Hines' dress.

Devers went from the breezeway to the basement.

There was a switch on a wall within reach and there was a naked light bulb suspended from the ceiling, but Devers did not touch the switch. Instead, as he invaded the dark, he waited for the boy within him to come out of hiding. And he moved into the dark past, beyond the oil burner, the dusty trunks, the sleds, the garden tools, the snow shovels, and the lawn mower until he came to the clothesline. At both poles, as his bowels stabbed him, as his bitten fingers pained him, he undid the knots and rolled up the waxed rope.

Suddenly the air stank of carbon monoxide and in the silence he heard a Buick engine choking and coughing in a garage behind a house in Flatbush.

In the nightmare dark Forrest Devers stalked the boy who had come out of hiding and who was trying to escape to the dreaming dark of the American Theater on Fort Hamilton Parkway in Brooklyn, in the Brooklyn of no more, west of never, and a canyon and a pass away from the savior in the saddle who was William Farnum.

Close to where Nancy Glaviano and Mag Devers were hanging and licking the dark, he grew a third gallows tree. After he had created a horse, he bound the boy's hands and lifted him into the saddle. He fitted the belonging noose about the boy's neck, stepped away, and struck the flesh of a flank.

The horse bolted. The branch bent. The tree was not inclined.

Monday, June 3, 1968

ONE

Devers had one eye on Mag, the other on Jane Russell.

After the Late Show, *The Revolt of Mamie Stover,* came the Late Late Show, *Enchantment,* starring David Niven. Weary of the pitchmen, he shut off the seven-inch Sony.

He found a book and studied the Contents: "Frank Asks Questions," "A Ghastly Subject," "An Irresistible Temptation," "A Game of Bluff," "Frank's Revelation," "The Plot," "Spreading the Snare," "The Haunted Room . . ."

"September was again at hand, and the cadets at Fardale Military Academy . . ."

Frank Merriwell's Chums by Burt L. Standish, copyright 1896 and 1902 by Street & Smith. EX LIBRIS EMRICH VANBROECK.

Again Devers went to Mag. He stroked her hair and returned the cornsilk. He took her pulse and spring was again at hand at the University of South Carolina.

He returned from the kitchen with a quart of milk, a wedge of wedding cake, and the Sunday *Times.*

Helen Keller was dead at eighty-seven. *Olavhalsolem, requiescat in pace,* Lord have mercy. Lord have mercy on those blind who are not blind, those deaf who are not deaf, those dumb who are not dumb, those fingers that touch and do not feel, and on those who are alive and do not live.

The Vietcong clung to a foothold on page one, along with

Charles de Gaulle, and with Kennedy disputing McCarthy on war in a TV discussion.

Retreating to the sports section, he read Joe Nichols' story on the Belmont Stakes, Arthur Daley's out-of-season insight into pro football and agreed with the observation that baseball's heroes were in the past, football's heroes in the present.

When he turned to Leonard Koppet's story on the new Big League math, he thought of Miles, of Charlie Spencer, of the fuck-you money, and of Curtis Buchanan's farewell to him: *Goodbye, Mr. Devers. Mr. Alderholt will be in touch with you.*

He went to Scotty Reston's column about the passing of the old generation in politics, and about the belief that Kennedy was the man to beat and that the issue would be decided in California. After he had read Russell Baker's column concerning the anatomy of a failing lobby, he glanced at Mag Devers.

He withdrew to the *Times Magazine.*

In the table of contents his bloodshot eyes caught "The Haunting of Robert Kennedy" by Victor S. Navasky, and then were captured by a nine-em cut of Bobby and Jack. The caption read: "There are a ghost, a shadow, an image and specter in Robert Kennedy's race for the Presidency. The ghost is the memory of John Kennedy (above, the two brothers at the White House, 1963). The shadow is . . . But see Page 26."

He turned to the page and was instantly drawn to Page 27 and the half-page cut of Bobby standing under a poster of Jack as he spoke at a 1966 political rally. And then he read the excellent article.

Jesus Christ and John F. Kennedy, two pictures on a wall of a room in a flat of a tenement in a Detroit slum, and a picture of John owned by a retired Rock Island Line railroad man who could not understand why they killed him who was so good to everybody, and Bobby ain't Jack but his brother's brother, we loved him, and will love Bobby, for the Kennedys have a lot going for them, and there is not only unconscious guilt, but conscious guilt, for one of us killed President Kennedy.

He fled to the nature editorial and the last sentence he read was: "June, summer, quite possibly Eden for a little while."

Devers understood that the Eden of a little while could be banished from June as the Camelot of a little while had been banished from November.

The night hung on, the hours dangling on a gibbet with Nancy Glaviano and Mag Devers.

TWO

6:50 A.M.

The telephone's first ring did not rouse Mag, but it returned Devers from the cannonade at Fort Donelson.

"Hello," he whispered to anyone but Grant or Buckner.

It was Teller.

Devers unlatched the front door and admitted a member of Nancy Glaviano's funeral. Neither said anything about a good morning as they marched to muffled drums to the den.

Done with his examination of Mag, Teller trailed Devers out to the breezeway.

"I'm off to Cypress Hills."

"Thanks, Mel.'"

"Did you take the rope down?"

"Yeah."

"Did you doze off?"

"No."

"You can flop down, Dev."

"Where?"

"With Mag. Where else? I've got my funeral for this week."

"Anything special you want me to do?"

"Sure, something very special. Keep her alive and wanting to stay alive."

"How would you do that if you were me?"

"That's a good question."

"What answer have you got for a schmuck who laid a virgin?"

They were at the front door before Teller, visibly upset, said, "You lied to me last night, huh?"

"Yeah."

"And you just told me the truth because you want to share my guilt with me. Right?"

"Right."

Teller sighed. "The truth? Was it worth it?"

"As of now, no. As of then, yes."

"*Boychik,* I don't think you're ever going to lie to me again."

"Probably not."

"Can you lie to Mag?"

"Must I lie to her?"

Teller meditated on it. "I'm not you. Mag's not Ruthie. Mag's more like Nancy Glaviano. That's what you have to remember."

"Shall I tell her you were here twice?"

"Not unless you have to. And you might have to. I don't know." He found the doorknob before he turned to Devers again. "Ruthie thinks you had indigestion. I told her to stay off the telephone and stay away from here today. If you have trouble, call my office. If you don't get an answer, it's because I'm laying my nurse."

"Joke?"

"A funeral's a tough act to follow. And if I'm ever going to start futzing around with my nurse today's the day. June 3, 1968. A fucking lousy black day."

"I noticed at dawn."

"You Irish bastard, you owe me a drink."

"For sure."

"I'd take it now. Only I'm driving."

Devers followed Teller out. "Nice car."

Teller observed the sky. "Nice day. So what's the score?"

Devers, who had once predicted Strontium 90, Man 0, said, "June 3, Fuck U. 2."

"It's the right score, but I liked it better when you were picking Once Over Lightly." Teller turned to Devers. "Here's one for you. Life Over Death."

"I'll give you six points."

"Keep Mag in the den all day. Talk it out, drink it out, sleep it out. Hide the scissors, the razor blades, and don't let her lock the bathroom door. Not until you're sure."

"How sure can I be?"

"You bastard. If I knew, I wouldn't be on my way to a funeral."

THREE

The telephone woke Devers. Not Mag.

"Hello."

"Dev? Hank."

"Greenberg? Bauer?"

"Alderholt."

Hank for Henry, honey for sting, newsboy for general counsel. Alderholt of Northwestern for Buchanan of Pennsylvania. Horatio Alger versus Frank Merriwell. Scripps-Howard was Hank's bag, and in it were two black pebbles.

"Buchanan said I'd be hearing from you."

"Did I wake you?"

"You did, and I thank you for it. I dreamed I was Charlie Spencer in my Maidenform teeth."

Alderholt laughed and laughed.

"Sing out the message, Hank."

"The message? Disregard the previous telephone call from Cleveland."

"What does that mean?"

"Dev, I had dinner last night with Curtis. And we got to talking about—"

The interruption was caustic. "The message, please."

"Curtis will forget if you forget. Curtis will forgive if you will forgive."

"And then what?"

"Life goes on."

"As before?"

"Very well put, Dev."

Devers persisted. "Before Charlie Spencer?"

"It was admirable of Charlie to assist the father of the bride."

"Hank?"

"Yes, Dev."

"Tell Curtis to go fuck himself."

Unabashed, Alderholt asked, "And do you have a message for me?"

"Yeah. Start dictating a letter. To the effect that we amicably agree to suspend the contract between us."

"Effective July one?"
"It's June three."
"You do have fuck-you money, don't you?"
"Any other questions, Hank?"
"I have some answers for you. Very interesting answers, I might add."
"The message, Hank."
"It is June three. Devers, Buchanan, and Scripps-Howard make three. I need not tell you which of this trinity matters."
"The message, Hank."
"You profit us by appearing five days a week in—"
"The message, Hank."
"You could profit us more by appearing seven days—"
"Hank—"
"—a week and we have no objection to Spencer assisting you even on those days—"
"What's in it for Charlie?"
"Tell me what *you* have in mind."
Devers observed the sleeper and roused his own attention. "Right this minute?"
"Yes, Dev."
"Let Charlie take over the column. And let me out of the contract."
Alderholt coughed. "In the Cleveland symphony orchestra—hell, Dev, we'll take Charlie. But only if he plays second fiddle to you."
Devers said nothing.
"Dev, is that understood?"
"Yeah, Hank."
"Now, dear friend, how can we help Charlie?"
"Good question. Now top it with your answer."
Alderholt did.
Devers thanked him for Charlie.
"One thing, Dev. You call Charlie and tell him to get to

work on a 'Dear Dev' column for tomorrow's papers. Tell him to write how grand it feels to be working with old pals Dev and Curtis. How Curtis was big enough to let bygones be bygones and invite him back after reading the Belmont column. Tell him to admit it was union troubles, strikes—"

"Charlie won't buy it."

"Will he admit television killed us?"

"Yeah."

"Will he confess in his column that he was wrong about Curtis being a Wall Streetwalker, Frank Munsey back from the dead, a Red-baiting—"

"Hank, he's a Bircher."

"Dev, dear friend, I know Charlie wasn't lying when he quoted Curtis as saying the *News* was an American newspaper beating all the damned New York foreign-language papers. But damn politics. Scripps-Howard is what matters to me. Does Charlie matter to you?"

"About Charlie and me. How about a Daley-Lipsyte arrangement? Four and three."

"We're selling Forrest Devers. Seven days a week. It's your business how many 'Dear Dev' columns a week—look, if Charlie stays hot, we may have you writing 'Dear Charlie' columns."

Devers listened to Alderholt laugh. He agreed to telephone Charlie, to take Charlie with him to Los Angeles on Tuesday, to Cleveland on Wednesday.

Farewell, Horatio Alger. Charlie thanks you.

Mag slept on.

Devers was dialing Wild Turkey, smashed dentures, and shattered glasses. One ring, one bright hello, and he wondered whether he had a wrong number.

"Charlie?"

"Good morning, Dev."

A glance at Mag told him otherwise. "Is it really that way in Rockville Centre?"

"You hung over?"

"Little bit. How about you?"

"Son of a bitch, you know there's something to be said for ginger ale. You go to bed smiling about Hartford and wake up in the morning and it starts all over again. The smiling about Hartford, I mean."

"Nice town."

"They love you in Hartford. I think I forgot to tell you that yesterday. And I think I forgot to tell you—you Jew bastard—that *I* loved you in Hartford yesterday. And I love you this morning."

"Is the Hungarian whore sitting on your head?"

"The hell with her. I've got Hartford."

"Charlie, what are you doing this morning?"

The cheer, surprisingly enough, was sustained. "Right now I'm working on the boy's book. You know, the Jesus Christ who was born in a manger named Miller Huggins." Devers rallied his attention. "Anyway, I'm going to work right up till noon. Then I'm going out for a hamburger and a milk shake. And then I'm going to have the Belmont column Xeroxed. Going to make a hundred copies. And then I'm going to get to work on finding the kind of work I should be doing. I've got my Ayer's directory and I'm going to mail out the column to one hundred newspapers, anywhere and everywhere in the country. Do you read me, Dev? I want to get back on a newspaper. Geography no object, salary no object. I just want to find some dinky press box and hear and smell some dinky press running over what I've batted out on some dinky typewriter. Do you understand me, Dev?"

Devers understood more than he had hoped to understand. "Yeah, Charlie."

"I was talking to Izzy Title last night before we left the party. And Izzy was telling me how much he hated Jolson, but that if Jolson came back from the dead and was looking for a piano player he—Izzy, that is—he'd get up early in the morning to be first in line to beg for the job. And you know why? Occupation's the thing. *Occupation.* And he said this, too. It didn't have to be Jolson, it didn't have to be the Palace. Just any old piano, just any old singer, just any old place where a guy is singing, where a piano needs a player, where people are listening."

Charlie was smart, Devers was dumb.

"Do you hear me, Dev?"

"I hear you."

"I figure—what the hell—I can live without New York, without Toots Shor, and even without Forrest Devers. If I can find myself some newspaper where—Dev, do you understand me?"

"Yeah, Charlie."

"I mean what I'm saying. Even if it means covering the local bowling leagues and YMCA basketball."

"Yeah, Charlie."

"Anywhere, anyplace. Even Springfield, Mass. Now any old guy who'd go back to his hometown with his tail between his legs has got to mean what he says when he's talking about occupation. Right?"

"Right, Charlie."

"Don't humor me, Dev. This is too fucking important to me. And I'm too fucking old to lay around and dream for miracles. Hell, ball players go back to the minors after they can't get around on the fast balls. No disgrace, is it? A ball player's got to play ball as long as he can, and a guy who wrote sports—look, it's not like I'm going back to Hanover and trying to break into the Dartmouth backfield again. Is it?"

"No, Charlie."

"No cracks?"

"No cracks in your armor."

"You like the Xerox idea?"

"It's a great idea."

"But what, you Jew bastard?"

"Don't throw your teeth at me, Charlie."

Charlie was not amused. "Fuck you! I'm hanging up unless you've got one more slaughterer's knife under that fucking Jewish gabardine of yours. Come on, stick it to me."

"Shut up and listen."

Charlie listened. Mag listened.

FOUR

"I hate you," she said.

"They love me in Rockville Centre. In Cleveland."

"I hate you."

"I love you."

"I wish I'd killed you first."

Devers said nothing.

"I may kill you yet!"

Slowly Mag arose. She was rushing toward the breezeway when he intercepted her.

"Let me go!"

"Where do you want to go?"

"Out of your room. Out of your sight. Into *my* house."

"There's nothing beyond the door. There's no house anymore. The Devers family doesn't live there anymore."

"Stop looking at me."

"Blanket your charms."

Returning to the bed, she pulled the blanket over her head. Her anguish rent the blanket. "Why didn't you let me die?"

He sat down at the desk, and his voice sat down upon his heart. "You are dead."

"I wish I were."

And he said to the blanket, "You are. The dead return to the land of the living for twenty-four hours. That's known as God's mercy. If the dead choose, they can return to life because God knows they'll surely—sooner or later—choose to return to the dead."

"I choose to return now. Right now."

"Twenty-four hours. God's rule."

The blanket spoke no more. And Devers made no sound as he stole from the den to the kitchen and to the refrigerator. He filled a tall glass with ice cubes and with a diet drink, and then he returned to draw the blanket and expose a gray head and dark eyes.

"Sweet poison," he said, extending the glass to her.

She took it. "Tab!"

"Tab is for the living, for the weight-watchers and the girl-watchers. It's Coca-Cola. Coke, the registered trademark of the drink of the discriminating dead. The dead lose weight no matter what they eat or drink."

She drained the glass. "It's Tab."

He took the glass from her before she could break it and slash her throat. "Can't fool the dead. Got to make a note of that."

"I'm not amused."

"Got to make a note of that, too. The dead aren't easily amused. Would you like some bread and cheese?"

"No."

At his desk, he turned to Mag again. "How about a Salem?"

"Why are you keeping me here?"

"Me keeping you? It's the dead who trap the living. And I know why."

Mag was slow to evince interest. "Why?"

Devers let silence weave more intrigue as he recalled his Saturday morning visit with Karen and his dark Sunday morning entombment with Mag. He recalled Karen's questions and his own surrender of long-kept secrets. He recalled Mag's questions and his own evasions and his ploy of sex.

It was different now, beyond nightmares. Death flirted with Karen, but Mag was flirting with death. Perhaps the poison of the past was the one antidote to remedy Mag's rage to die. He had to try, he had to succeed, if only to win a Pyrrhic victory. He could chance losing Mag for himself, but he could not chance losing her to death. He wished to raise her from the dead, to leave her free to go anywhere but the way of Nancy Glaviano.

Devers went at it with resolve, but in his own way. He was grinning before he engaged Mag. "We're going to play a game. God's favorite game. The dead versus the living. Questions versus answers. Truth versus lies. Secrets versus revelations. Great game. Like Twenty Questions, only the dead aren't limited to any number of questions. They take all the truth they can take, and all of God's laughter they can take."

Mag was attentive but bitter. "The Jewish God?"

He baited her. "Is there another kind?"

"Ask your sister."

Devers stayed with banter, certain Mag would tune him out and tune in her own three-o'clock-in-the-morning ghosts. "Karen doesn't know. My mother knows, but she has no more time for me. Early this morning I got hungry for matzo-meal pancakes with sour cream and strawberry jam. But my mother didn't hear me. I think, ever since she died, that she's been taking her Catholicism seriously. Well, I guess it'd be pretty tough to canonize someone who spent the hereafter messing around with matzo-meal pancakes." He lit a cigarette. "My old man hated them. He liked buckwheat cakes, maple syrup, butter, and pig sausages on a Sunday morning. I did, too. Mr. Vanbroeck liked Sundays because it was the day he played the Baron of Brooklyn to the Brownsville sash-and-door crowd, held in check and screened by my old man. Little pig sausages. The meaning of Sunday long after the dream of meaning."

Mag said, "I'm not listening to you."

"Why should you be? I know God's order. Bring back answers. Twenty on rye, two on whole wheat and hold the—"

"Oh, shut up!"

He did. The trouble was Mag was still shut up. After some minutes, when it seemed to him that Mag was dozing off, Devers reached for the telephone and dialed for the correct time. Hearing the voice of a girl computed to be a girl, he said, "I beg your pardon, I don't understand a word of Hungarian." It was ten-thirty-seven. "No, that was no lady you saw me with last night. That was you." He glanced at Mag. She was as dead as vaudeville. "My wife? I'll tell her. At the next séance."

No reaction. He quit. The whiskey was sweet and warm and disconcerting.

The telephone came alive. He let it ring three times to wake the dead.

Devers' voice was computed for joy. "Hello."

It was Teller. "Everything all right?"

"Yes, God. She got back just fine, and she must be all right. Tastes the difference between Coke and Tab."

"Some funeral. I'll call you tonight."

"Thank you, God."

"You drunk, Dev?"

"I'm on my way, O Lord."

"You doing this for Mag?"

"Yes, Lord."

"For God's sake, Dev, save her."

"Farewell, O Lord."

A long count and then: "Who was that?"

"God. Who else would the Lord be? God is one."

She pouted. "If you won't answer a simple question, how can I trust you to answer questions that aren't simple?"

"All questions are simple."

"The answers, too?"

"Once you know them they're simple."

"Who did you call earlier?"

He told her.

"Who just called you?"

"Mel Teller."

"Why?"

He told her about Teller's two house calls.

"I don't believe you," she said. "If what you said was true, I'd be in a hospital now."

Devers told Mag why she was not taken to a hospital. She listened, but she did not understand.

"I took eighteen seconals."

"That's short of the world's record."

"Did I—did you make me throw up enough to be sure?"

"Mel cheats his patients. The bottle held twenty-five capsules. Twelve seconals, thirteen placebos."

Her stare was severe. "How long have you known this? How long ago did you tell Mel I wasn't to be trusted?"

"I didn't know a thing about it. Not until Sunday morning." He told her about Nancy Glaviano, and she listened. He told her about Ruthie Teller, and she did not listen.

"We have a basement. And a clothesline."

"No more clothesline."

Mag understood and said nothing.

"I won't give you any placebos. I'll give you nothing but the truth. You're dead. The truth can't hurt you. It could save you."

"I want to die," she said with terrifying calm.

"Truth to go, the secrets to go. Take them with you to your grave. Let them dig your grave. Let them poison and hang you. You're out of seconals and rope."

Mag turned away from him. He watched and waited. Soon she turned to him again. He saw the hate and it was good. He heard the first question and it was good. For a beginning.

"Did you sleep with Letty?"

"I did."

"Did you get her drunk?"

"She was drunk and hysterical when she crashed the party I was having with Donna."

Mag looked sick. "What party with Donna?"

"We'll get to that. It was the low point of the party, and I damn Letty for ending the party at that lousy, low point."

"I'm losing interest in Letty. I'm concerned about Donna."

"Next question?"

"No." Mag paused. "Same question. How could you seduce that poor girl?"

"I meant to scare her. I told her I'd fuck her if she didn't go to bed. Alone. In Donna's room. She asked for it."

"And you couldn't refuse! Fifty-one years old! Father of the bride!"

"Maybe that had something to do with it. I was angry with the bride."

"You were stupid!"

"So I was. The pain wasn't worth the pleasure. She gave me the stink of her vomit. Her fear of God."

"Just once?"

"Just once."

"For pleasure?"

He chose other words. "Release. Desire. Lust. Anything but love. I was hungry for her."

"You had me the night before."

"No, Mag, I had Letty."

"Oh, God!"

"It's not pretty, but it's the truth."

Mag was forlorn. "Of course. I'm not pretty anymore. Letty is."

"Letty doesn't remind me of your mother."

Mag, given the opening, refused to take it. She instead pursued the same question. "Does Letty remind you of Donna?"

"She can. She didn't last night. She helped me, for a short while, to forget Donna. And myself."

"What exactly did you do with Letty?"

"What a boy does to a girl, what we did when we—"

"I don't believe you! I believe you did more! All those disgusting things you could never make me do!"

"Not true."

"What stopped you?"

"As Charlie says—"

"Don't tell me about Charlie! I know about Charlie."

"One game at a time, as Charlie says. Letty said she was a virgin."

"Oh, God! You're sick. A dirty old man like Charlie. A pervert." Mag's voice died away.

Devers did not refute her. He took another drink and another step into his conscience. "In the beginning there was my mother, and then there was my sister, and then my wife, and then my daughter. Four women whom I love, and only one of whom I'm allowed to give the fullness of my love. I've dreamed the forbidden. Of my mother, my sister, my daughter. Dreams remembered as nightmares."

Mag burrowed under the blanket. Long minutes later she emerged. "*Why was Donna so upset when she left?*"

The second question. As sickening as it was, Devers preferred it to the agony of Mag's silence and withdrawal.

"I upset her," he said. "I meant to upset her."

Mag prompted him. "Are you too overwrought to go on?"

"No."

"What did you say to Donna?"

"I told her she did wrong. But I was wrong to tell her she did wrong. Because the wrong had been done, couldn't be undone, never would be undone. And—what the hell—I had no right to talk to her as if she were still my daughter. She's Herbert's wife. She's his problem. Like you're mine. And I'm yours."

"What wrong did my little girl do?"

And Devers detailed the drama and the riddle of the two black pebbles before he drew his conclusion. "She cheated. Donna knows she cheated, and she knows I know she cheated, and she knows I don't like it, and I don't like her for cheating. And, worst of all, I don't like what it'll do to her and her marriage. What a man does to a woman and what a woman does to a man doesn't add up to perversion and can be as sweet as you want it to be. But to cheat, to come up with an answer you couldn't have come up with in a million years, that's perversion."

"I don't like that word," she said.

"It doesn't matter what you like, Mag. It doesn't matter anymore if you like Donna or if I like Donna. The smaller question is whether Herbert keeps on liking Donna. And the larger—the *largest* question is whether Donna can go on liking Donna."

"How many drinks have you had?"

"Does it matter? The answer's not inside the bottle. It's

outside. If you spill whiskey on a pebbled beach, you can always look into the bottle and see the color of the whiskey you spilled."

"You're drunk."

"Not yet."

"You're sick."

"Like daughter, like mother. You whisper nothing but sweet perversions in my ear."

She failed to understand what was never meant to be understood. "What do you mean—'like mother, like daughter'?"

"Correction. I said—'like daughter, like mother.'" He poured again. "I know the color of the whiskey. It's the color of truth if—"

"Answer me!" Mag was sharp, and Devers was pleased she was.

Directing the sharpness to his mind, he said, "The answer? There are eighteen capsules, all of them the color red. Some are sweet poison, some sweet life. Now pick up the telephone and place a call to San Francisco. Ask for Miles. Ask him to give you the mathematical formula by which the black pebble of death falls to the path and the white pebble of life is nowhere to be found."

"That's no answer."

Devers thought about it. "You're right. It's no answer. Maybe it's a question or a group of questions. Something like this: to be or not to be, to die or not to die, to go to Dallas or not to go to Dallas." Lord have mercy, Lord have mercy, he said to himself.

Mag brought him back from Arlington. "You said something about Donna and me. What is the truth about my daughter and me?"

"You don't like Donna, she doesn't like you. You haven't liked her for years, she hasn't liked you for years. So the hell with her and Herbert because—and this is the sickening truth—I don't like her, haven't liked her for years, and don't ever expect to like her again."

Mag was gasping, the truth was choking her. "Did Donna tell you last night she didn't like me?"

"We didn't talk about you. We didn't have time. We had Letty on our hands. And not soon enough. I have more guilt about Donna than about Letty. Much more. I should have listened to Donna and laughed. I should've shut up. Fuck you, Frank Merriwell. Shut up, God explained. Yeah."

They were both quiet for a while until Mag posed the third question. "*What did Miles tell you about Herbert?*"

Devers liked the question, the sequence, and the train of thought taking Mag to the ultimate question.

"Miles thinks Herbert's a prick."

Mag winced. "That's not what Miles said to me Sunday on the phone."

"Did you expect him to? Did you expect him to tell you he was sick for having introduced Donna to Herbert?"

"Why did Miles give Donna the answer to the riddle?"

"He never suspected it'd been posed by Herbert. Donna hated Herbert the first time she saw him. Miles couldn't believe she was dating Herbert."

"Donna lied to me," said Mag. "She said she was very much impressed with Herbert the first time they met in Miles' apartment. She did admit she never expected to see him again. Because he was so superior—" She broke off. "She lied."

"She's still lying. To herself."

"Miles lied."

Devers now spoke up for Herbert, but Mag was no longer interested in him.

"Does Miles like me?"

"He loves you."

"Does he like me?"

"Yeah. When he's in San Francisco, and you're in Valley Stream."

She wanted to cry. "He can't stand me, can he?"

"Not when you mother him. Especially not when you try to be a Jewish mother."

For the first time, Mag sat up in bed. She bared her breasts and her torment. "You know why! You know who made me that way!" She fell back, but not to silence. "There's always been a secret understanding between you and your children and your mother. I hate you all for it."

Devers let it pass. Instead he tried to control her with another kind of understanding. "You need an occupation."

She was bewildered. "Occupation? What are we talking about? I thought we were discussing Miles."

"Fine. As long as we discuss Miles the mathematician. Not the holes in his socks, the frayed shirt collars, or the lack of meat on his bones."

Mag glowered at him. "May we discuss Miles the—the—I can't even bring myself to say it."

"What are you afraid of, Mag?"

"All I know—and I really don't care to know it—or believe it—all I know—in my heart—is that Miles is mixed up in something."

"Something what? Something evil?"

"Detrimental. Yes, detrimental—"

"Nice big word."

"—detrimental to himself. To his future. And to his country."

"Is his country your country?"

"What?"

He repeated the question.

"It's our country, his and mine."

"Sweet America?"

"I don't like that phrase. I hate it. It reminds me of your mother."

"Do you doubt my mother's love for America?"

"Your mother's country wasn't my country."

"What do you call your country?"

"My forebears were settled in South Carolina before the Revolution. I had three ancestors who bore arms against the British."

He remembered the Civil War. "Also several who bore arms against the United States of America."

"We're Americans! And I didn't declare war on Miles! He declared war on me! On every blessed thing I stand for!"

"What do you stand for?"

"You know what I stand for. And you know what I can't stand."

"*Ramparts,*" said Devers.

"You read it and I'm stupid enough to believe you don't like what you read."

"I try to understand Miles."

She understood nothing. "He's ruining himself in San Francisco."

"Maybe he's got a reason. A cause."

"He belongs in Berkeley. You said so yourself. Miles the mathematician."

"He does only if he decides it's the place for him. Not because you or I think so. That's the meaning of sweet America: to be free—"

"I don't care about it!"

"Do you care to hear about your brother Miles?"

Mag went from bewilderment to indignation. "Don't you dare say anything against him. I wish my son Miles were more like him."

"How do you know he isn't?"

"I know, I knew my brother."

"Did he ever confide in you about Spain?"

"Spain? What's Spain got to do with anything?"

"Do you remember the Spanish Civil War?"

She did. "What about it?"

"When your brother graduated in 1935, he wanted to go over and join the Loyalists. The Republicans fighting Franco. The Fascists."

Mag did not believe him. "Who told you that? Miles was going to Knoxville for an interview, for a reporting job on the—" The name of the newspaper evaded her.

"The *News-Sentinel.*"

The past overwhelmed her. "He was killed. Driving my father's Ford. He missed a curve in North Carolina."

"Your mother blamed herself."

"My mother!"

"Your father told me. He wasn't happy about Spain, but he wasn't about to stop Miles. Your mother asked him to stop Miles. He did. By arranging the interview in Knoxville."

Mag gasped and was silent for a while. "When did my father tell you this?"

"Late in August, 1937. I was back in Columbia, working for the athletic department, going in and out of offices on Main Street, peddling football season tickets. I met your father coming out of *The State*. He asked me—"

"When did you first meet my father?"

"November, 1936. In *The State* city room. He congratulated me on a sports column I had ghosted for the football coach. Don McCallister."

"Why would my father tell you something so personal about Miles?"

"We went into Central Drug for dopes. Jesus, when was it we started calling them Cokes instead of dopes? Anyway, he had something very urgent to ask me."

Mag was intrigued. "What was that?"

"He wanted to know if I'd be interested in coming to live at his house."

"I wish you had said no."

"That was my first answer. I had a room, rent free, in the field house. It suited me."

"Why did you change your mind?"

"Your father pointed out some advantages. I was over twenty-one, and by having a city address and a job waiting for me on *The State* when I graduated, I could claim residency in South Carolina, and not have to pay the out-of-state tuition fees. Also, he offered me your brother's room, meals, laundry, dry cleaning."

"What did my father think he was getting in return? A son-in-law?"

"He laid it on the line."

"Did he now?"

Devers took another cigarette. "First he told me about Miles and—"

"You told me."

"Then he talked about your mother. Her guilt, her depression. He was afraid for her, afraid of her. Of her delusions. She was blaming him. The car killed Miles. She was insisting she had wanted Miles to take a train or a bus. Not so, said your father."

"Didn't my father tell you the house was dirty unless we girls cleaned it and you never knew we were going to have dinner unless we cooked it?"

"He did."

"It didn't frighten you off, did it?"

Devers shook his head.

"What did my father tell you about me?"

"He told me about his three daughters. He was worried the least about Catherine. She was strong, and her life centered on herself and the boyfriend she had at Carolina. Janet, the youngest, was a problem. Doing poorly at Columbia High. She missed Miles the most. Margaret, the eldest and prettiest, worried him most. He blamed Carleton Dabney—"

"You knew! And you never let on until that day I told you everything!"

Devers shut up. He waited for the ultimate question or a question leading to it. Mag said nothing. She wept all the way home to South Carolina.

He tried again. "Sweet America. My mother broke free and went to Barnard. She broke free again when she married—"

"I don't care to hear about your sainted mother!"

"You broke free. You came to New York."

Mag glared at him. "How unhappy did that make your mother?"

"My mother hated you. She had cause. You made her son happy. Her husband fell in love with you. You gave her two grandchildren. A brilliant son, a beautiful daughter."

Mag was wary. "Did she ever accept me?"

"The truth is she loved you."

"I don't believe you."

It was time for the absurd. "She loved you because you were always so happy."

"Happy? Your mother never made me happy. She made me unhappy."

"What's a mother-in-law for?"

The question failed to turn Mag southward. "She made me afraid of the telephone, the doorbell. When I'd see her, when I'd hear her, something—" She gave up the old anguish.

Afraid of losing her to sleep, Devers struck at Mag again. "My mother was stupid. She had no idea of real happiness. Your Dixie kind of happiness."

Mag was back. "Dixie?"

"Happiness in Dixie is feeling faint at the breaking of a

raw egg. Armies of ants marching over dirty dishes in the sink. Rancid butter. Moldy bacon. Dirty diapers."

"I hate your mother. I hate the memory of her."

"How about the memory of *your* mother?"

She would not be baited. "We're talking about Miriam. When did she first learn about me?"

"The first letter I wrote home from Pendleton Street."

"What did you say about me?"

"I said I was behind, three to two. The three opposed to me and my intrusion were Mrs. Griffin, Catherine, and Margaret. True, wasn't it?"

Mag was cold. "Yes."

"But not the whole truth. I never told her how I used to notice you on the campus. So forlorn, so beautiful. So alone, even in the gaggle of your sorority sisters. I knew your name, from your picture in *The Gamecock.* I never asked about you."

"Why not?"

"I didn't have to. You were—you and Catherine both—were whispered about to me."

She frowned. "What kind of whispers?"

"The best kind. You were Miles Griffin's sister. Miles was a *Gamecock* legend. Hildy Johnson and Walter Burns in one tall, handsome package."

Mag wept for her brother before she found another question. "When you fell in love with me, did you write and tell your mother?"

"No."

"Were you in love with me?"

"Can you ever forget how much?"

"Have *you* forgotten how much I loved you? Why didn't you write and tell your mother—?"

"You didn't tell your mother," Devers said.

"How could I?" Mag demanded. "You were living in the house, on the same floor, using the same bathroom. You were so close. I used to have such real dreams of you stealing into our room, past my sisters' beds, and into mine."

"I had erotic dreams, too," he said.

She uttered a truth with shame. "I took care of you."

He remembered the lie of Mag's virginity, the truth of his desire, the care of his release, and her caution. South Carolina was a dry state. Dry fucking only. So went their honeymoon joke.

Returning to his task, Devers said, "I took care of your nightmares."

Mag held the nightmare look. "Don't remind me."

"I have to. That day in the drugstore your father told me about—"

"Please!"

"—the kids harassing you and your sisters. Climbing the tree outside your bedroom window in the evenings when your father was gone from the house, when there was no man about the house to scare the kids away. Your father told me about Tyler Lattrel exposing himself and—"

"Shut up!"

Devers shut up. For Mag's sake. For the sake of Tyler Lattrel whose parents had to put him away in various institutions before a grave covered his sins and the sins they had visited upon him. The poor, feeble-minded offspring of Phi Beta Kappa parents.

"When you came to New York," Devers said, "I told my mother you were chasing after me."

Mag fumed. "You wrote me! You told me you'd be happy to see me."

Devers found himself remembering how unhappy the Lattrels had been to see him, dragging their son home, and confronting them with their shame.

Mag had to prompt him. "Didn't you?"

"I was going into the Army. I thought we might have a nice

time together. So I answered the letter you wrote to Greensboro."

"I'd never been to New York."

He remembered the idyllic day. "I never should've taken you to Ebbets Field. The beauty of you traipsing barefoot in the outfield grass did me in."

Mag remembered the tension of the day. "Before you took me home from the game, you called your mother. What did you tell her?"

"I told her I was bringing home a girl who was, in three days, going to be her daughter-in-law."

"That surely didn't delight her."

"No. She was unhappy. Only because Karen couldn't be there to meet you. But she was very happy about you. She was a teacher, you were a teacher. She looked at you and saw what beautiful grandchildren you'd give her."

Mag was pensive. "I liked your father. We loved each other at first smile. Not your mother. I never was quite sure what was behind her smile. After that, it was easy for me to learn to hate her."

"You hated her because she taught you how to be a mother to your children."

"I had my own mother to teach me!"

Devers took the opening. "What did your mother teach you? The folly of going to New York and returning pregnant? The fate of being a war widow? The shame of having a child sired by a New York Yankee Catholic Jew? Jesus, it meant nothing to her when we named our kid after her dead son. It took your father to teach you something. He put you and the baby on the train. Because he loved you and me and Miles."

He lost Mag. She slipped away under the blanket, under the pillow, suffocating memory and truth.

Devers stood up. The wrecking ball swung and struck him.

He staggered to the bathroom, ran water over his head and face, and wasted no time.

The bourbon tempted him and he succumbed. The bed tempted him, but he knew that sleep was Mag's escape. Not his.

He sat at the desk, smoking, thinking, giving Mag a long count. Once she rose again, he meant to hit her again and again.

The telephone rang. A faraway sound from a house now so far away. The breezeway was too long for leaping, too broad for escape. He listened to the ringing until it died and gave way to the roar of a jet. The sky had not fallen.

He went to work. He dug up graves and found unknown addresses. The actors gathered, he built two sets, two scenes. He ran through the scene in Raleigh, and then the scene in Columbia. The progression was wrong. Columbia came before Raleigh, the hotel coffee shop before the bedroom closet.

Devers was considering the effect of putting Raleigh before Columbia, 1939 before 1938, when he saw the blanket slipping away, the pillow falling, and Mag stirring in her sleep.

Lord have mercy, Lord have Tuesday. He wished a sweet dream for Mag. The nightmares were to come with her waking.

FIVE

The sun was June noon high. In the shade of the breezeway, Devers stalked back and forth between the closed door to the house and the open doorway to the hideaway until he heard the telephone on his desk ring.

He hurried inside, saw that Mag was awake, and picked up the telephone and his voice. It was Karen.

"Karen! How are you?"

"Much improved. So much so that I was permitted to call you."

Devers did not allow Mag's stare to cloud his smile. "And who said Mondays were blue?"

"You sound well."

"I know the secret. Wake up to a good breakfast of wedding cake. I'm going to try it for lunch and dinner. My heart's as light as the cake."

"Was it a nice party, Dev?"

"Nice but flawed. By your absence."

Karen wanted to hear all about it, and Devers reported a lie: it was as nice as those Saint Pat parties he used to give in a time before parties were buried in Arlington. He gave her humor, nonsense. Mag gave him an evil eye. Karen laughed.

Done with laughter, Karen asked about Donna and Herbert. "Did they make their flight to Washington?"

"Took a plane. Honeymooners forget that they themselves are lighter than air."

Karen laughed. "I love you when you're ridiculous."

"The wedding cake's lighter than air."

Karen was reflective. "*Mon Dieu,* such a wonderful surprise yesterday to behold Donna and her husband. Let no one quarrel with me about the efficacy of prayer."

"The Verrazano Bridge is a prayer."

"Yes." Karen's mind was elsewhere. "Do you like Herbert?"

Devers lied. "Very much."

"He's not your kind of man."

He did not relent. "He's like Miles."

"Is he? Truly?"

"He's his own man."

"Herbert never said a word about you."

He had to be ridiculous. "I guess I've lost him to Donna."

"Or vice versa?"

Devers laughed. "You are *the sick one.* It's not your heart, it's your head."

Karen persisted. "I asked Herbert what he thought of you. He responded, at first, with a very strange look, as if I were impertinent in asking the question, or in believing he so much as gave you a single thought. He answered me only because of Donna's presence."

Devers said, "I don't care what he said."

"Herbert said you were a proper father-in-law."

"Great! That's like winning another Pulitzer."

"I didn't consider it a proper answer. But, for Donna's sake, I let it pass as one."

"God love you."

"I tried to call Margaret earlier. There—"

"I gave Mag the day off. And Lord help me when I get the bill from Lord & Taylor's."

"Yes, may the Lord help you."

After Karen said something about Sister Alicia wanting her to end the call, Devers told her he hoped to see her on

Saturday. He told her about his forthcoming trips to Los Angeles and to Cleveland. He was thinking about Raleigh and Columbia, but he wanted to leave Karen laughing.

"You remember Primo Carnera, the giant Italian, the former heavyweight champ. Well, later he became a wrestler. And when he went to Los Angeles for a match, a sportswriter asked him: 'What do you think of Los Angeles?' And Carnera replied: 'Los Angeles? I pin heem quick.' "

Karen laughed. Until Saturday.

Mag was heard from. "Lord & Taylor's, indeed."

"A white sale. White lies."

"What did Karen say about Herbert?"

"She believes she loves me much more than Herbert does."

Mag said nothing. She had learned about Herbert. It was in Devers' voice and eyes. He tried to interest her in brunch. She was not interested. When she left the bed, she made straight for the bathroom.

Devers was right behind her, keeping her from shutting and locking the door, watching her. When she was done, she moved past him slowly before she broke for the door to the breezeway. His reaction was quick. He caught her in the open doorway, pulled her back into the room, kicked the door shut, and pinned her to the carpet.

He played the clown. "Mag Devers? I pin her quick."

And then she was free to return to bed, to claim the Sony and the escape of a seven-inch soap opera.

For the twenty minutes Mag watched the Sony, Devers watched her. During a break for a commercial, she turned to him, turned off the set, and stayed with the drama in his eyes.

"When did you stop loving me?"

He derided it as a soap opera question.

"You stopped loving me when I came out of the hospital."

The question pinned him quick. He was not prepared for it. He stalled. "Which hospital?"

"The last hospital," she said. "The hysterectomy."

He was saving his whiskey for Raleigh and Columbia, but he needed a shot of it now. He had not counted on a third blast of truth's poison. He took the drink, another cigarette, but he was unable to speak.

Mag prompted him. "Nothing to say?"

Aware that silence was working against him, he said a lot that told very little. "What is there to say? You went to the best hospital. Harkness Pavilion. You had the best surgeon. Dr. Albert Riddell. The operation was a success. The tumor benign. We were happy with the news. You recovered well. You looked well. You felt well. In six weeks you went back to Dr. Riddell and he told you to go on as before. With your sex life. We went to make love, you and I. And it turned out one of us was still sick. Me. I was impotent."

Mag heard the sad song. "Why? It wasn't anything physical with you. What was it?"

It had all been very simple. Jacob Wald the butcher would have appreciated the surgeon whose scalpel was as sharp and unflawed as his skill. The tumor—large enough to qualify for the baseball museum in Cooperstown—and the uterus were separated from Mag's flesh with the ease of a strand of desire being removed from a glass of chilled wine.

But there was an effect, a reaction of flesh severed from flesh, felt by Devers' own hands, heart, and loins. Even after six weeks, Mag's flesh—especially her breasts and beautiful ass—was something other than flesh. It was putty. Putty fresh from a tub. But Devers was no Pygmalion, Mag was no Galatea. The putty was more quicksand than ivory.

The bedsheets were fresh, the nightgown raised above the breasts was silken and strange, and the perfume was as sweet as sugar pine. But, as he touched her, his hands and his heart sank, and his desire was a moon that never rose.

The whiskey in Devers clabbered, the heart in him faltered, and he prayed, not for an impossible surge of potency, but for a possible recession of his nausea. It was all he could do to keep from fouling Mag with his vomit.

Devers now gave Mag the medicine Mel Teller the general practitioner had brewed from Sigmund Freud's unread tea leaves.

He said, "It was all in my mind. You were ready. I wasn't. Your legs were spread, you were warm and inviting. I wanted you, the boy hiding within me wanted you. But there were things on my mind. Left there by Dr. Riddell. A tumor, a uterus."

Mag was appalled. "You're sick."

"I was," he confessed. "Sick to death with the deepest fear of my life. With the one question that left me punch-drunk."

"What question?"

"Is Mag dying of cancer?"

Good word, "cancer." Good soap opera word. Mag swallowed it, and the medicine worked. For a long while she brooded in silence, her eyes leaving Devers and retreating to the past crisis.

There was silence, and Devers saw that it was good. He had no wish to reduce Mag to putty, not even in his hands. He was going for blood and flesh, muscle and drive, awaking and singing, rising and shining, off and running.

As for himself, Devers remembered things best forgotten, especially the jokes. He was afraid the surgeon had left his scalpel in Mag's vagina. How many circumcisions could he stand? It was no longer funny, the comedy was ended, the comedy was a soap opera. He appreciated the irony, he whose lampooning of soap operas warmed many of his winter columns.

Biding his time, holding the train to Raleigh and Columbia, Devers picked up a copy pencil, some sheets of copy paper, and tried to find respite in sketching out a column. He was back on the Scripps-Howard payroll, on the beam. His mind took him from Drysdale's shutout drama to Zero Mostel's comedy.

He was scribbling notes when he heard Mag's voice.

"How many girls did you sleep with before you married me?"

The question, it seemed to him, was as inane as his column notes. Yet he saw it as an obstacle which might derail the train to those truths that could save Mag.

"That's a helluva question to put to Frank Merriwell," he said, facing Mag.

"I asked you."

"Are we talking about sex or love?"

"Sex."

He dropped the pencil. "I used to belong to a very select club. You were expelled if you masturbated. The first time I masturbated was in a Brooklyn hospital after I broke my right ankle, after a nurse gave me—"

"Get to my question."

"Are whores girls?"

Mag winced. "I don't want to hear about prostitutes."

"Would you care to rephrase the question?"

"There must have been some girls or some girl before me."

She was right. Right in Columbia there had been one of Mag's sorority sisters. Beverly Fullerton. She had her own car, her own Trojans in the glove compartment, and her own pleasures on the back seat. Hey, Forrest, like a ride home? The long, lovely way home. To Pendleton Street. Hey, Mag! Come and get your runaway Yankee slave! Bye now! A wave of the tennis racket to bring innocence to her sweat. Came the special train to Orangeburg. Bye, Beverly. Hello, Mag.

Devers shook his head. "Whores. In Brooklyn, in Manhattan, in Easton P.A."

"What about Columbia?"

He thought about the whores sitting on the balconies on lower Main Street, across the street from the university. "They used to whistle at me. I blew them kisses. From afar."

"Greensboro," said Mag.

"Ah, Greensboro. I lived in a bawdy house."

"It was a *boarding*house. And the girls weren't prostitutes."

"You're right. I was wrong to think so." It was a truth he had been slow to learn. "They were girls from the country, the mountains, the backwoods. Nurses and typists and secretaries thrilled by indoor plumbing and store-bought clothes. By excitement and doors that opened all the days of the week and made every night Saturday night. I hardly recall their names. Such good names, such good faces gone bad so quickly."

"Did they take money from you?" asked Mag.

"Only what they had to borrow. And they paid back. No, they used to come to my room—or other guys' rooms—and they let you know what they wanted. If they asked you for a cigarette, they just wanted to talk. If they asked you for a drink, they wanted to go to bed with you. Oh, for the days of Green River. Fifty-five cents a half-pint. If you were out of booze, you were out of luck."

Mag listened. "What did you talk to them about?"

"I listened."

"What ever made you regard them as prostitutes?"

"They gave their favors to any earless, heartless oaf with booze in his room." He went to Omar the tentmaker. " 'I wonder often what the Vintners buy / One half so precious as the stuff they sell.' "

Mag was confused. "I can understand the quotation. Especially from an alcoholic. But what has it to do with the girls in Greensboro?"

"Liquor. Liquid currency. They did it like minks, and drank like fish."

"How do you drink?"

"The story of my drinking would make a book as thick as my Irish head."

"You love it, don't you?" It was an accusation.

He studied the bottle of Wild Turkey. "It's not Green River. You can sip it."

"It's not wine."

"No, it's my life-blood."

"You and Charlie."

"Name a game I missed or a column I never wrote because of my drinking." Silly argument, at this time. He found a smile and a way out. "Charlie says the Irish in me drags me into the bar, and the Jew in me drags me out."

Mag was not amused. "After you married me, what other women did you sleep with?"

A wrong-way question. He was going south, Mag was taking him north. He did some thinking about north and south before he dropped a name. "Florence Rosenfeld."

Mag's reaction troubled Devers. No shock, no rage. The surprise was unpleasant rather than unsettling. The ensuing questions were clinical. When? Where? How? Why?

His answers were frank and straight, his details telegraphic.

The Rosenfelds' house-warming party. 1954. The downstairs guest toilet was occupied. He went upstairs and tried the bathroom door. It was open. Occupied. Florence Rosenfeld was stuffing something into the hamper. He apologized and tried to retreat. She detained him, asking him to check the lock on the door, which had not worked for her. He fooled with it and fixed it. She told him he deserved a kiss, and she gave it to him. And then they fooled with each other. Yes, she kissed him *there.* Yes, he kissed her *there.* And, yes, it happened again in Mag's house. 1955. The Saint Pat's party. The second and last time. For the next day Florence Rosenfeld telephoned him at the *World-Telegram.* So much for her.

Now Mag demanded that he name the other women with whom he had been involved.

Devers had no names to spill. The names he told her were of strange cities in foreign lands. The Olympic trips. The fun was over. He was not looking forward to Mexico City.

Mag did not believe him. September would find him in Mexico City, her in a cold grave.

Devers fled from Mag's grave to the graves of the Civil War dead. The resolve of his frontal assault on Raleigh and Columbia was weakening. He was no longer Grant, he was McClellan, looking for excuses instead of the enemy. He became Stonewall Jackson and executed a flanking maneuver to capture Columbia for Mag.

"About Florence Rosenfeld—"

Mag was quick. "I don't care to hear any more about her."

"I was using her—"

"You used each other."

"—to get into the subject of friends."

"She's no friend of mine."

"Good. You won't miss her. I can't think of anyone you'll miss. The parties are over, the friendships are over. Time you thought of returning to where you now belong. Columbia, South Carolina."

Mag said, "I don't care where I'm buried."

"Is Columbia dead and buried? Are your sisters dead and buried? Are the schools destroyed? Your occupation gone?"

"Which occupation?"

"Well, you're dead as a wife to me. Dead as a mother to Miles and Donna. You're not dead as a schoolteacher."

Mag had nothing to say, something to ponder.

Devers went on. "This house is dead."

She turned on him. "You killed it. The night you moved into this room."

"You chased me from our bed."

"Is the Chinese girl dead?"

Devers shook his head. "I remember. Hal Groves' party. I was drunk, too damn drunk, feeling too damn old—the hell with it. Nevertheless, you chased me."

"For the night. I didn't mean for you to move in here."

"True," he said. "But this is also true. The bedroom had become a tomb. I was glad to be free of it."

Mag said, "Free of me."

"The dark side of your moon."

"You could have slept in Miles' room. At least you would have been in the house."

"I couldn't," he said, and said no more.

"You walk into your son's room as if it were a museum. A national shrine."

Devers did not bother to refute her. Instead he told her what was true to him. "The whole house—every room in it—was a morgue."

"Since when?"

"Since Christmas 1966, when Donna, home for the holidays, said it was."

"Sass," said Mag.

"Out of the mouths of babes. The hell with it. We'll sell the morgue. The real estate agent'll sell the house, and another generation'll buy a home. Next stop, Columbia."

"Don't bother," she said.

Devers said nothing. He acted. He reached for the telephone and got Mag a seat on a jet leaving La Guardia airport Tuesday morning at nine o'clock. He was telling her about it and she was not listening when the telephone rang.

It was Mel Teller. Checking in, checking up, checking signals with Devers. The next time the telephone rang Teller would be five minutes away from leaving a bucket of fried chicken on the front doorstep.

Devers returned to Mag. "Guess who's coming for dinner? Colonel Sanders and a Southern-fried chicken."

"Was that Mel?"

"*Doctor* Teller."

"I'll miss him," she said sadly.

"Don't make him miss you the way he misses Nancy Glaviano."

"I won't use his pills."

"It was rope. And it wasn't his." He said no more. He bided his time, waiting for the telephone to ring, and for Mag to care enough to ask the crucial question.

Devers leaned back in his chair. Sleep leaned on him.

SIX

A night train. The warning bells at a crossing roused Devers. His ears opened to the telephone, his eyes to the twilight, and his adrenalin to the horror of Mag trying to escape.

He blocked her at the door to the breezeway. She turned

back. He turned back to the moment when, certain Mag was asleep, he had let down his eyelids and his guard.

The ringing stopped. He picked up the telephone and heard nothing but the pounding of his own heart. Teller was on his way. Mag was not. Teller was on the ball. He was not. He was more angry with himself than with Mag.

Devers lit a cigarette, stood up again, and put the whiskey bottle away. Aware of his imminent problem, he paced the floor. He recalled one of those mathematical puzzles Miles used to confront him with: how the missionaries got the cannibals across a river in one canoe. The problem now was getting to the front door and the bucket of chicken without leaving Mag alone.

His scenarios failed him, the flaws and dangers surfacing easier than the solution. He had given up on the chicken when a rapping sound reached him. No reaction from Mag, from reality. He was sure the sound had risen in his strained mind. He paced the floor a few more times before he allowed himself to unlock and open the door to the breezeway.

At the foot of the door he saw a large paper sack. He picked it up, examined the contents, and thanked Mel Teller, the graduate of Nancy Glaviano's Basement Medical School.

Without a word, without a thought of how Teller had opened locked doors, Devers returned to the desk. He tore the sack apart to draw Mag's attention. Succeeding, he went on to announce the menu: fried chicken, potato salad, cole slaw, biscuits, honey, cherry tarts, milk.

"Shut up," Mag said.

He did. He arranged food on two paper plates.

"Who was that?"

Devers glanced at Mag. "Mel Teller. The invidious, invisible Jew."

"Aren't the doors locked?"

"They are. Maybe it wasn't Mel. He would have brought chicken soup."

Mag frowned. "Keep your jokes and your food."

"Good. I can't trust you with either one. You might decide to choke yourself on a chicken bone. I wouldn't even trust you with a cherry tart."

He sat down and ate. It was a task at first, but then a taste of the chicken brought on nostalgia and hunger. The hunger was good, the nostalgia better. For he had an idea it could work for him.

He tried. He did a monologue.

"Fingerlickin' good but better for memory-licking. Remember the Orangeburg County Fair? 1937. Remember the fried chicken after the football game? What a twilight it was, what a dawn it really was. The calliopes and fried onions and the wind at the sawdust. The new moon climbing. Oh, Christ, how I feed on that day. Red letter? No, orange. Orangeburg, an orange, harvest moon. And the train, the special train, how special it was. Our first date, first day together. You didn't want to go. You'd been to the Orangeburg Fair game in 1935. With Carleton Dabney."

Mag was listening. She heard the name.

"Your father had to talk you into going along with me. I was going alone. I was *The Gamecock* sports editor and I had to go. No matter, you came along, we went together. And how well we did. How much we had to tell each other. Going to Orangeburg, talk was easy, kidding was hard. Hey, Margaret, where's Carleton? Dixie humor as raw as Green River whiskey. You wanted to cry when the oaf moved down the train aisle to spread his Southern Comfort. Remember me taking your hand, squeezing it, and letting you know that you weren't alone with Carleton, that I was with you? I got you to talking about him, and by the time we got to Orangeburg, you knew where Carleton was, and where he wasn't."

Mag was on the train, in the past. He held her there.

"Good game, good day. And the train back to Columbia, sitting on the tracks, held up not by Jesse James, not by the moon. But by us. By you asking me how I had come to this place, this hour. And I told you about Frank Merriwell and Emrich Vanbroeck, about Jack Fallon and Yale, about my father and Princeton, about Devers & Son."

Devers remembered that he had not told her everything. The train had begun to move, the fun had begun in the cars, and he had ended with the tragedy at third base at Erasmus Field. He had never gotten to Jacob Wald.

He went on. "You asked how I felt when I broke my ankle. I told you. You wept because you understood what it was to be so young and so afraid of life and living. My feelings, I said. My feelings, you said. Take Orangeburg, two broken hearts, one moon, song after song, train smoke in our eyes, a smashing of all light bulbs, a dark train, laughter, and the wonder of being in the eye of a dream."

He was still eating. He brought out the whiskey. He needed it now. He thought he had captured Mag and he was not about to lose her.

"We held hands, we sang. I kissed you, you kissed me. I was in love with you, you were in love with me."

Devers said no more. Mag had been there. She was there now, he hoped, he prayed.

Mag was heard from. "What is the eye of a dream?"

"A dream come true. For one minute, an hour, or, at the most, a day like Orangeburg."

"At the most?"

"That's the way it is with dreams. Like the passing of the moon between the sun and earth. How long does an eclipse last?"

Mag thought about more mundane things. "I can't even believe Orangeburg anymore. You went away to Greensboro, you never sent for me."

Devers said nothing. He waited for a question.

It came. "Why did you leave? Why didn't you send for me?"

Devers got up. He went and sat down in the leather chair. It was more comfortable, closer to Mag, closer to the door to the breezeway. No desk, no food, no whiskey between them.

"You asked two good questions. I'll answer the second one first."

Mag was wary. "Why?"

"If I give you the answer to the first question, you may miss getting the answer to the second one. I don't want to hold out anything. I don't want you to miss—"

"Shut up and tell me!"

Devers took Mag back to the past. It seemed correct to him. A train moving from the present to the past would arrive at 1939 before it came to 1938.

"September, late September. 1939. Late on a Saturday, after a night football game I was covering. Wake Forest versus South Carolina at Wake Forest. I'm in the Sir Walter Hotel in Raleigh. In the lobby. I'm listening to Enright telling us a story about Rockne when I feel a slap on my shoulder. It's Russ Joyner. Joyner of South Carolina. He's drunk and the guy with him is drunk, and Russ introduces the guy with him who needs no introduction because he's the one and only Carleton Dabney."

Mag came to attention.

"More bullshit about South Carolina, the football game, how great I'm doing in Greensboro. Then Russ hollers to someone, disappears in the lobby crowd, and there I am face to face with Carleton Dabney. He invites me for a cup of coffee. I try a lame excuse. It doesn't work. He's got to talk to me, and I go with him because it suddenly hits me that Carleton Dabney is dying to sit down and tell me about Mag Griffin."

Mag heard her name and wept.

"We sit down in the coffee shop, and I wait for him to hit

me with the sad news that he's going to make Mag Griffin Mrs. Carleton Dabney. But he begins by telling me nothing and asking me a lot of questions, deep-down questions that drunks ask on a Saturday night. Do I know who he is? I do. When was the last time I saw Mag Griffin? I tell him. Do I write to her? I do. Does she write to me? She does. But I don't tell him it's a long time between letters from North to South Carolina. Next question. Do I love Mag Griffin? I do. Does Mag Griffin love me? I think so. I hope so. He bums a cigarette, and then he asks another question. Do I know what happened between him and Mag Griffin?"

Mag died.

"I tell him I don't know what happened. Did I know that he and Mag Griffin were once engaged to each other? Yeah, I knew. Am I interested in hearing what happened in Greenville? I make a crack about Greenville, but he isn't laughing and he isn't asking questions anymore. He's telling me something, and he isn't telling it well, not because he isn't glib like a good law student should be, but because he's drunk and a little broken up about a girl named Mag Griffin. But I'm listening and wishing I were drinking bourbon instead of coffee because it's a horror story he's telling me."

Mag heard him and died of horror.

"He's telling me about a Saturday night in Greenville. The night after the South Carolina–Furman football game. He's telling me how you drove up from Columbia with three sorority sisters. How he took you to the game. How much fun you both had. How you were supposed to spend the night with an aunt of one of your sorority sisters. He's telling me how he got you away from a party, and how he took you to the Meadows Hotel."

Mag heard the name of the hotel and mistook the blanket for a shroud. Devers rose and ripped away the shroud. When she tried to use the pillows for masks, he tore away the masks.

Her body and her tears were naked as he stood over the bed.

"The Meadows Hotel. A side-street hotel. Carleton Dabney's got the room key in his pocket, and there's a stairway to the second floor, and to a room with a bed, a bottle of 5-Crown, and a little tin of condoms. He's telling me about the two of you drinking. The two of you undressing each other. The two of you getting into bed. And he's telling me how he's on top of you and into you and the fucking is just great when someone begins to bang on the door. He's too scared to say anything, and he hears the country voice of the house detective ordering him to open the goddamn door before he goddamn busts it in. He tells me how you run into the bathroom, how he opens the door, and tries to bribe the house dick with five bucks. But the house dick isn't about to be bribed. He's a big, fat, dirty slob and he pushes past Carleton Dabney, opens the bathroom door, and leers at Mag Griffin as she's struggling with her pants. The dirty man doesn't move until the girl and the boy are all dressed, and then he marches them out of the room. Tells them what a respectable hotel the Meadows is, and tells them they can consider themselves lucky that he's not the kind to report them and have them kicked the hell out of the university."

The dead wept on.

"I hear you, Mag. And I can still hear Carleton Dabney telling me how he walked the streets of Greenville with you for hours before you could stop crying. Yeah, I can hear him telling me that when he said good night to you at the house where you were spending the night with your sorority sisters he knew he was saying goodbye to you. That the engagement was over, that there was no chance of either of you forgetting about the Meadows Hotel, the house dick, and the sickening shame of it all. Because—and the drunk had tears in his eyes now—he was remembering how much he loved you and how much you loved him before there came a knocking on the door."

Devers turned about too quickly. The room wavered. He found the leather chair. He had to sit down before he fell down. His voice did fall.

"End of report on a happening at the Meadows Hotel. End of tears. Dabney of South Carolina has a question. What happened between Mag Griffin and me? I say nothing. He tells me what he's heard around Columbia about me living in your house. About the romance between us. He repeats the question. But I tell him nothing. Except I've got to be moving along if I don't want to miss my car ride back to Greensboro. I pick up the check. And he picks up my ears by telling me how he's going to marry a girl from Charleston who goes to Winthrop. I congratulate him for nothing, because the Winthrop girl means nothing to him except good sense. Good family, well fixed. Carleton still loves Mag Griffin. But how the hell could he marry her and spend the rest of his life knowing she knew what a dumb, cowardly bastard he was."

Silence for a little while. Then more about Carleton. From Mag.

"Carleton didn't tell me he was taking me to a hotel."

"I believe you." He did. He always had. She never lied when she told him everything. But her measure of everything was not his.

Mag faltered. "When—when we passed the hotel—the Meadows Hotel—we were on our way to a restaurant—Carleton—all of a sudden—at least it seemed so—asked if I'd like to drop in and have a drink with a few of his law school friends."

"Carleton didn't tell me that. But I believe you."

"I loved him."

"I'd never question that."

Mag withdrew. "What would you question?"

"Look," he said. "I don't mean to cross-examine you. You asked a question, and I thought—"

"Say what you think!"

"Carleton was stupid for taking a single room. He should have taken a double, registered both of you, as man and wife, and the two of you would have had a good life together."

She took it the wrong way. "Do you believe I would have gone up to a hotel room with Carleton if he had?"

"No," he conceded. "But you did go up to the room with Carleton. Did you ever ask yourself or Carleton what had happened to his law school friends?"

"What do you think?"

"All right, you did. Then what?"

"Carleton told you what happened."

"I'm trying to get your side of the story."

Mag scowled at him. "You won't get it."

"I got it. I understood it a long time ago. I married you."

The scowl persisted. "Why did you go to Greensboro?"

He was McClellan again, rallying his forces, playing with logistics. "You were graduating, looking for a teaching job. The chances were against your finding one in Columbia."

"I did find one."

Devers found another reason. "South Carolina wasn't Princeton. I wasn't playing baseball and football. My Frank Merriwell dreams of college were gone."

"You talked it over with my father. You decided to finish school. What changed your mind?"

"Your father gave me the pros and cons. He hadn't forgotten his own son. He wasn't about to push me in any direction."

"What were the pros and cons?"

Devers hesitated. "He said I could get my degree and it would mean nothing to me. But, if I didn't get my degree,

I'd make too much of not having it. He spoke from experience, having gone from high school to a weekly newspaper. He also believed I might come to regret not having four full years of college. The best four years of a man's life. He knew. He had shared Miles' four bright years at Carolina."

Mag's scowl was gone with sorrow. "Yes," she said to herself.

"Your father did say that Carolina had very little to give me. What the hell, as he put it, I had the best education in journalism. I was a graduate of the New York City newsstands. He couldn't think of a better sportswriter in the South. He was sure I was going places. Greensboro was just a stop on the way back to New York. He was more proud of me than my own father was when I made the *World-Telegram.*"

"What did my father say when you told him you were staying on?"

"He smiled. He said he liked having me around. I was good for him. For you."

She tried not to cry. "What changed your mind?"

Devers took care. He took Jacob Wald's perfect knife in hand, and he tried to remove the soul of truth from the past with the ease of a strand of cornsilk hair drawn from a haystack.

"I couldn't stay at your house any longer."

"Who said so?" Mag asked.

"Nobody but me. Something had happened. I had to leave the house. I had to get out of town."

Mag paled and trembled. Her voice was hollow. "Janet."

Devers shook his head and waited for Mag to find the truth.

She was wild. "Not Cathy?"

Again he shook his head.

She was still wild. "Who was the girl? One of those sluts on *The Gamecock?*"

It was time to ready his voice. "No."

"Who?"

Gently, gently. "A poor woman—now resting in her grave. A good woman made mad by another grave—her son's too early grave."

Mag listened, she heard. And the thunder deafened her, the lightning struck her dumb.

Merde! Shit! Devers heard God and dropped Jacob Wald's knife. Softly, softly. Painfully, painfully. The words were stones passed by Devers.

"May 22, 1938. Late afternoon. I'm walking you and Cathy to your sorority meeting. Then I stop by the library, pick up a book, and return home. The house is quiet. I know your father's at *The State,* and Janet's down the street with the Wagner twins. I look for your mother. No one in the kitchen, nothing cooking on the stove. I go upstairs to my room. Your brother's room. The room is empty. The closet door is shut. Two of the four drawers in the bureau are open and empty. Not my two drawers, but the two bottom drawers. The drawers your mother warned me not to disturb. Because they contained shirts, underwear, socks, and handkerchiefs belonging to her dear dead son. I remember smiling and telling myself that your mother was trying to tell me something. That I was welcome to the four drawers. And that she would welcome me back in the house when I returned from Brooklyn the following September.

"Then I hear a sound. A sob. From inside the closet. My smile goes. And I rush to open the closet door. And there's your mother. Sitting on the floor. Sobbing and clutching your brother's things. Her graying hair wild. Her eyes red. Her hands wildly bringing up the mess of shirts and underwear and biting them. Kissing them. And biting them again. She sees me and tells me that Miles is dead. Flash, bulletin, what happened on a North Carolina highway in 1935 is happening again in the closet. I sit down on the floor beside her. I let her talk because I think talking is good for her. And she talks. She damns your father for giving Miles the Ford to drive to Knoxville. She damns God for taking her beloved son. She bargains with God. She offers her three daughters for the return of her son. She weeps. She groans. She bangs her head against the wall. I grab her. She weeps on my shoulder. She rants on. There was no boy like Miles. No boy ever. You're a nice boy, Forrest. A good boy, and I'd like you and maybe love you like my own son if I knew that God had sent you to me but I know you were brought here by my damned husband and I don't like you and can't like you and never expect to like you and I don't believe what my damned husband says when he says you're brighter and smarter than Miles because nobody was ever smarter or brighter than my Miles.

"Then she asks me, are you brighter than my Miles? And I say, no, Miles was the brightest and the best. And she keeps repeating, yes, yes, yes, yes, yes, yes. And she begins to claw me and tell me how much she misses Miles, how she hates her damned husband, how lonely she is for Miles, how unhappy, how tormented, how forsaken. And her hands are moving. Tearing at her old dress. Ripping it. I try to stop her. To quiet her. She is at my mouth with her mouth. She's over me with her hands. She pulls my face down to her breasts. She tears my shirt, tears at my belt buckle, buttons, zipper. Love me, love me, love me, she keeps crying—"

His eyes upon Mag, he watched her and her sudden rage. The Sony, hurled with both hands, came at him. He ducked. The Sony glanced off his right shoulder, hit the floor, and dented a closet door.

Devers did not feel the pain in his shoulder. The deep pain came when he beheld Mag as she turned into Susannah Yarborough Griffin, and then into Nancy Glaviano.

Certain she would make another move, he watched her, saying nothing, doing nothing but thinking about what he had said and what he had left unsaid.

He wondered if Mag remembered asking her mother, in

the long days that followed, why she was dressing up every morning as if it were Sunday, and why she was using so much lipstick, rouge, and perfume. He wondered if Mag now recalled his own long, strange absences from the house.

Mag rose. He rose. She went to the bathroom and returned to the bed before he sat down again, this time at the desk. He was too close to exhaustion, too close to sleep, to return to the leather chair.

Devers turned on his desk lamp. Mag reacted at once. She asked him to shut it off. He did nothing. Night had fallen. The lamp fell as a book thrown in anger by Mag found its mark. The lamp was not broken. The book was. For the sake of the books, for Mag's sake, he straightened and darkened the lamp.

Devers smoked, picked at the food, and sipped nothing but milk and waited. He watched the dark, unable to tell whether he was seeing a lady curled for sleep or a tiger crouched for springing.

SEVEN

The telephone in the dark house rang. At his desk, in Mag's jungle dark, Devers heard it as a ghost of a sound. Eerie. Nostalgic. Like waiting at an airport and hearing the faraway wail of a train whistle.

The fucked-up and fucking past. The hell with Raleigh and Greenville and a closet in Columbia. The hell with anywhere but Orangeburg.

The telephone rang again in the house.

Christ, had he made Mag understand Orangeburg? He remembered trying and failing, separately, with Miles and with Donna. Orangeburg was too near to be captured by Miles' telescope. He saw the harvest moon as a zero moon. Zero was the wheel that made mathematics go. By itself, the moon was zero. With the sun and earth the moon had meaning.

Third ring.

His and Mag's Orangeburg was too far to be reflected in Donna's mirror. She had her own Orangeburg, and her own rage: the massacre of black students, black February 1968. Black year.

Fourth ring.

Devers had never revealed the big truth of Orangeburg to Miles, Donna, Mag, or to himself. He did tell Miles and Mag about the singing on the train. Why the hell had he forgotten to tell them that he had not sung since Emrich Vanbroeck had forsaken him, and that Mag had not sung since Carleton Dabney had forsaken her?

Fifth ring.

The fucking closet. Had he told Mag the truth about it? Was there a truth to tell and was he privy to it? Was it a closet or an open grave next to Miles Griffin's grave? Devers knew enough to damn himself. Indecent exposure was just that, in a tree, in a closet. Lord have mercy on such as Tyler Lattrel and me.

Sixth ring. Who the hell was calling?

The hell with the house. Why not Columbia? Where else could Mag lock hands with her sisters and light up the skies. It was jet time, Columbia time. You can get to anywhere if you start out from somewhere.

Seventh ring. Who's not giving up?

The hell with telephones. Face to face, heart to heart, he

could not reach Mag. Between the speaker and the listener lay Babel.

There was no eighth ring.

Devers went from the seven rings to the wedding ring on Donna's left hand. Was it Donna? He dismissed the thought, but not his last dialogue with his daughter. Who the hell was he to cry shame to Donna? Why was he so angry with her? Her truths angered him, her lies angered him. Why was the anger there? And wasn't it there before the truths and the lies? Hadn't the anger grown up with Donna?

Karen was wrong. Wounded king, hell. He was the wounding king. Lord have mercy, Lord make me dumb.

He reached for a cigarette instead of sweet whiskey. As he struck a match, the telephone on the desk rang. He burned his hand in his haste to pick it up.

He put on a happy face that Mag could not see, a happy voice that she heard.

"Hello!"

"Dad?" It was Donna. Uneasy.

He played deaf to her mood. "Donna! How are you?"

"Where's mother?"

The happy face was lost, the happy voice was not. "Was that you calling the house?"

"Yes."

"Your mother—she's at the movies—with Ruthie Teller." His right hand was over the mouthpiece to keep Mag from Donna. But Mag was quiet.

"I wanted to be sure and talk to her first," said Donna. "You know."

He knew. He also knew he had no wish, at this time, to talk to Donna. What he had to say to her, he meant to put in a letter. To get the apology right.

Devers said, "When do you want your mother to call you?"

"In the morning. Between nine and ten."

"Good."

"How are you, Dad?"

"Fine!" He told her he was working on a column, getting ready to leave for Los Angeles in the morning.

"What happened with Letty?"

He was up to it. "She left late. I put her in a cab."

"That Gary Fallon," she said. "He was so drunk he got funny with me."

"Those Ohio State linemen, they know how to use their hands." He did not try to laugh. He was sure he could not make laughter.

"I wept at Arlington today," said Donna.

"I remember when it was a racetrack."

"Yes, Dad."

"How's Herbert?"

"He's sitting here, frowning at me."

"Good night, Mrs.—"

"Dad!" There was urgency now. "Don't hang up. Not yet."

Devers waited for the worst from Washington.

"I told Herbert the truth," she said. "About how I got the answer from Miles."

He was sick unto death. "You said Herbert was frowning."

"My husband was smiling until I tattled about Gary Fallon. Listen, Dad, Herbert never expected me to solve the riddle. He himself never did. I think it's because he never really tried. He doesn't go much for games and riddles. Anyway, the fact that I cared enough to ask Miles proved to Herbert that I was interested in him. And he loves me all the more for telling him the truth."

Devers was speechless. He had no ear and no tongue for good news.

"Dad, are you there?"

"Was this before or after Arlington?"

"After."

"They'll be hanging crutches there," he said absently.

His eyes were on Mag now. She was stirring, the blanket was stirring.

"Dad, am I forgiven?"

"I love you," he said to Donna. To Mag.

Mag heard him and surrendered stealth. Wild-eyed, she rushed to the door. Devers did nothing but press his hand over the mouthpiece to keep the clamor of Mag's escape from Donna. The fucking rope. Alexander Graham Bell's rope had him tethered.

His mind on Mag, his mercy on Donna, Devers stayed with his daughter, forgave her, told her he loved her more than he had the night she was born. She was his girl. He liked her. God, he liked her again. And wouldn't she please hang up now and tell Herbert how much she loved him?

Donna did. And Devers did, before he chased after a Mag long gone, far gone.

He went from room to room enlisting light in his battle against darkness and death. After his sweep had taken him to the master bedroom and had availed him nothing but specters, he beat a retreat to the rumpus room below and to the basement beyond terror.

But only Nancy Glaviano and Mel Teller were there, and he did not linger with the dead and buried and the alive and guilty. He took the steps upward two at a time and he was a long-distance runner gasping for breath and for hope when it occurred to him he had not searched closets and other concealments.

He felt he was losing his mind when he found himself opening the refrigerator door. The freezer. The washing machine. The dryer. The broom closet. The closet in Miles' room. The hall closet.

And then, with a hand that despair did not stay, he opened the closet in Donna's room and saw his mother-in-law huddled on the floor. He looked again, blinded his mind's eye, and saw his naked and wild-eyed ward.

He was weak on his feet. He wanted to lie down on the bed to take sleep's way out of a nightmare. But he sat down in a soft chair, found a second wind, and tried to gain Mag's attention.

She turned away and cornered her head to put him beyond her sight. The closet door remaining open, he threw her lines of communication, of life. He recounted the telephone conversation, he begged Mag to consider Donna's happiness and honeymoon. Nothing.

He tried to take Mag back in time to Orangeburg, to the moon and the singing and the awaking of their own lives. Nothing.

He dared to tell her about Miles' Zero Moon and he made sense. Nothing.

He tried to bring Mag forward in time to Columbia, to her occupation, their new house, their new life together. Nothing.

How do you explain the moon's orbit to the blind? Or tomorrow to the dead?

Mag considered nothing but emptiness. Rising and leaving the sheltering closet, she went to the bureau, jerked open the top drawer, clawed and flung bras, slips, panties, stockings, and socks. And then she attacked the suspended mirror, yanking it from its hook and smashing it against oak.

The mirror was shattered, but Devers did not stir. Alert to spring at her in the event she tried to use a sliver as a dagger, he watched her reach instead for a pair of panties. Because she was no longer the girl with the cornsilk hair, she strained and burst the elastic on the lard of her thighs and in the claws of her hands. She grabbed up a brassiere and ripped it before she bridled her overripe breasts. From the heap she chose a slip and broke the seams bringing it down over her head and over the swollen sheath of her hot and red skin. This done, she sat down upon the floor, chose nylon stockings, and ripped them as she drew them with abandon over her legs. Rising, she returned to the closet, jerked free a summer dress, and split seams bringing it down past her hips.

Devers watched Mag. He was not her keeper any longer. He was her audience and the show was on. The dirty show. The nightmare comedy. He watched her raise and rip the dress. He watched her shimmy and try to arouse him. Unmindful that the boy hiding within him was excited, he kept staring at Mag with another kind of pleasure: she was not dancing on the end of a fucking rope, she was not doing a death-rattle, she was alive and shimmying and kicking.

Mag laughed. She mixed her wild laughter with words. "Do you love me?"

He said nothing. It was Mag's act. And nothing he could tell her, none of his words, would mix with her laughter.

"Don't you want to love me?"

Mag turned from his silence and retreated to the closet's interior. She ripped dresses and coats from hangers hooked to the closet pole. She flung them to the closet floor, sank into the heap, faced Devers, spread her legs, raised her knees, and her voice.

"Make love to a whore! Make eyes at me like that house detective in Greenville! Make love to Mag the whore!"

Devers looked and listened. He did nothing to stop the show. It went on.

"Take it out, Tyler! Take it out and play with it! Look at me, Tyler! The shades are up and my vomit is coming up!"

Devers liked the show so far. The show of the past, the show of anguish, the show of life.

"Come into the closet! Your mother's waiting for you!"

He did not run to Holy Name Cemetery.

"Come into the closet! My mother's waiting for you!"

He waited for more.

"Come into the closet! Sister Antonia's waiting for you!"

The name is "Karen," he told himself.

"Come into the closet! Janet's waiting for you! Cathy's waiting for you!"

Bring it all up, get it all out, he told himself.

"Come into the closet! Your darling daughter's waiting for you!"

Devers was ready for it. He took it. He could take more. Mag lowered her knees and eyes. When she seemed to sink into the heap of clothes, Devers made a move. He reached for the telephone. As the sound of dialing reached her, Mag opened her eyes to rage.

"Who are you calling?"

"Cathy," he said.

"Wait till I'm dead before you invite her to my funeral!"

Devers was cool. "I want her to pick you up at the airport."

"The undertaker does that!"

Devers hung up the telephone. The test had failed. It would take more than a jet, more than a place to go, to save Mag.

He said, "It's not easy to die."

Mag's voice was hollow. "But it is."

"Death's a master of disguise."

She said nothing. She did not understand him. He had not expected instant understanding, or even delayed understanding. All he prayed for was her attention. And Death gave it to him.

"I know Death."

Mag knew him, knew his face, his voice. Knowing he was not lying, she listened.

"We met face to face. A black day in May, in the black year of 1933. Listen to the name of the street. Gravesend Avenue. The Brooklyn street of cemeteries, and of Erasmus Field, my high school's playing field. The dead in the graves beyond the right-field fence outnumber the living in the wooden stands. Emrich Vanbroeck lies dead miles to the west in a Greenwood Cemetery mausoleum. Princeton's a lost name on a lost map. In the stands are scouts from Brown, Colgate, and Fordham. Baseball—"

"I don't want to hear about baseball!"

"A game of death." He had her again, and he went on, dragging the cross of the day. "Erasmus is playing Boys' High. I'm playing defeat and the death of my dreams. Long season, hard season, good season at bat and in the field. And I've got a long football season ahead of me. My last two chances to win an athletic scholarship."

Mag again. "You didn't win one! I know all of that!"

"Not all, Mag, not all. It's the sixth inning. I've had two hits, made a great play at first base. Now I'm up for the last time. A curve hangs high. I swing and send it high and far to right field, high and far enough to carry all the way to Princeton or Yale." He paused. The pain of the moment was on him. "The ball hits the fence. I run hard and fast. I don't take the double. I go for three bases. I slide hard. The ground is hard. My spikes catch. My right ankle breaks. Multiple fracture. Bones and dreams."

Mag caught the catch in his voice, but she showed him no mercy. "You told me! On the Orangeburg train!"

Devers nodded and thought his head would fall from his shoulders. "I never told you this. An ambulance came for me. A policeman with a gun. In my agony, as I lay on the stretcher under the stands, I wished I were a horse so he could shoot me." He looked at Mag. She was looking, listening for something to hear. "They pick up the stretcher and carry me out to Gravesend Avenue. There's the ambulance. And there beside it, stands Death."

Mag was hearing him now.

"Death wears a black derby, a black suit, dark eyes, gold teeth, and a trimmed gray beard. And he carries a black cane. Death is an old Jew with tears running. Death haunts me in and out of the hospital. In and out of the three dead years that follow. I see old Jews and I look for Death's eyes and Death's tears. I have a long wait before I catch up with him. Or before he catches up with me."

Mag was with him. Hanging on his words.

"I'm with my father. Devers & Son. I'm in the mill and not in it. I'm carrying a large sheet of Florentine glass to the glazing stand. Three steps to climb. One misstep because I'm somewhere in a dead dream. The glass shatters. The pieces fall. A jagged section, with a dagger edge, rips cloth and flesh and hits bone. Between my shoulderblades."

Mag was heard from. "You said the scar was from a street accident."

"How could I tell the truth to a girl who couldn't stand to crack a raw egg?"

"I'm not that girl anymore."

"No," he said forlornly. "And I'm not the boy who looks for Death. Another ambulance, another hospital. Pint after pint of blood. Comes June, out of the hospital, back to work. A Monday. Lunchtime. I leave the mill and go alone to Pete the Greek. The Virginia ham steak is great. I'm eating at the counter when I sense something. Someone. I turn my head and almost puke. There he is. Death. Sitting next to me. Same black derby, same everything. But no tears."

Mag could not wait. "Who was he?"

"Death has a name. Jacob Wald."

Mag frowned. "Your grandfather! What kind of—"

"Shut up and listen," he begged her.

She did.

"He doesn't introduce himself right away. He orders a sandwich and tea. And I'm thinking to myself that my mind is playing tricks on me. All these old Jews look and talk alike. Then he turns to me and asks me how I feel. Good, kind question. I answer him with a hard look. Then he tells me my mother told him he'd find me here. I drop the hard look and he loses his old Jew look. I ask him about Gravesend Avenue and the ambulance. And he tells me he was there. He was there many times before when Princeton and Vanbroeck were alive, when I was alive and playing football and baseball. And he tells me he's seen my report cards, my medals, and he asks me why I'm not in college."

Devers had to find breath before he continued. "I can't speak, can't eat. He talks. About Einstein and numbers and mathematics. Do I know about such things? Not much, not enough. All I know is I had a dream of college, a dream of being a newspaperman. And both dreams were dead. He sips his tea and starts to talk about the time he was a bootlegger. He did his best business at the *Herald Tribune,* where he was known as Jake the Jew. So all right, he says, if you want to be an Irish *shikker* newspaperman, so all right. He hands me an envelope and I look at it and in it. A dirty envelope. Twenty-five dirty twenty-dollar bills."

No reaction from Mag, save bewilderment.

"September 21, 1936. Penn Station. My father leaves me, saying I'll never make it past Princeton Junction. And I'm standing there alone and afraid of the dead dream when Death comes to me. He hands me an old Remington portable that once belonged to a *shikker goy* on the *Herald Tribune* and still belongs to a *shikker goy.* I get on the train. It begins to move. I wave to Death on the platform. And Death blows me a kiss."

Devers said no more. He looked and listened for a response: a tear, a cry, a light in a lightless eye. He tensed as Mag made a move. She did nothing but raise her knees, spread her legs, and wait to be gang-fucked by ugliness, sickness, loneliness, emptiness, and a long line of dreads.

Tuesday, June 4, 1968

ONE

The note was on the kitchen table. By the light of dawn, at first glance, Devers read suicide. He had to read it again and again.

"4:30 A.M. DRIVING SOUTH."

He hurried out of the house to find that the station wagon was gone from the garage. He returned to the house and to the master bedroom. He opened closet doors and bureau drawers and saw that Mag's luggage and many of her belongings were missing from where she no longer belonged.

His mind'e eye saw Mag driving south on the New Jersey Turnpike, driving too slowly in the right lane. His mind's eye picked up a trailer truck driving too fast in the right lane until it struck the station wagon and scattered metal, glass, flesh and blood, and lit a cremating fire.

He went to the telephone and found confusion. He went to the living room and out of his mind.

Belt Parkway, Mag, onto the Verrazano Bridge. Regard the towers for climbing up out of the hell of things. Mag have mercy, Mag have mercy. Get out of the right lane, the Angel of Death waits there. Stay in the second lane. Get her up to fifty-five and keep her there. Stay in your lane, at your speed, on your route, and make it all the way home to Columbia, to your sisters, to the schoolhouse.

Keep your window open, Mag, let the morning ride with

you. Get the feel of the open road, the open sky. Chase the horizon over the hills and far away to yesterday, to tomorrow.

Look to the towers, Mag, and for God's sake stay out of tunnels, stay out of graves.

TWO

Eight o'clock in the morning.

Devers was sitting in the living room tracking the station wagon in Delaware when he heard a sound at the front door. A key sliding into the lock.

He saw Mag before the door swung open and revealed Mel Teller, calling his name in panic. Devers answered and went to him.

"The station wagon's gone!" Teller cried. "Where's Mag?"

Devers gave him the note. Teller read Devers' guilt before he glanced at the note.

"Where the hell were you, Dev? How could you let her get away from you?"

"I had to walk away from her. I'd said all I—said it all. I left her in Donna's closet."

Teller was confounded. "Where'd you go?"

"The one place I didn't want Mag to go. The basement. I stood guard outside the door. I sat guard—"

"You got drunk."

Devers shook his head. "Just dozed off. The dog in me slept." His voice cracked. "Got up at dawn."

"What have you done about it? What are you going to do?"

"Fly to Los Angeles with Charlie."

Teller sighed. He handed the key to Devers. "Put it back in the garage. It's yours. And put your brains back in your head."

Devers told Teller all about Charlie, and then he told him what he had to tell him about Mag. Teller listened and he sat down to keep from falling down.

"You did it," said Teller. "You're beautiful."

"She's a lousy driver. She's scared."

"Mag's daring to be brave."

"To be brave enough to kill herself?"

"No, Dev, no. I'm not ruling out an accident. But suicide? No." Teller was on his feet again. "I should've sent Nancy Glaviano to you."

Devers declined an invitation to breakfast and a ride to Kennedy. He accepted a B-12 shot, showered, shaved, dressed, packed, and made two telephone calls: he ordered a taxi, and he maintained order in Washington. He told Donna that Mag was driving south, and he convinced her that Mag had a brave, happy idea.

He was in Miles' room watching for the taxi and wondering about destinations. Mag had to reach Columbia. Charlie had to reach Los Angeles. For him Los Angeles was the dark at the bottom of the black velvet bag.

The two black pebbles. He remembered what Miles had told Donna to lead her to the riddle's answer. Turning from the window, he looked for his son and found him in the books on the shelves: Baseball Joe to René Descartes, Tom Swift to Albert Einstein, Red Smith to Baruch Spinoza.

Miles was no Herbert. He cared, he bothered, he looked after the sheep.

Devers never saw or heard the taxi. By the time he heard the doorbell he knew where he had to go.

THREE

The San Francisco-bound Boeing 707 was taxiing toward its appointed runway when Devers took off for 1958, for Valley Stream, the new house, the new life. He was standing with Mag and watching Miles and Donna cycling down the winding street when Charlie Spencer slapped his shoulder.

"Dev, can't read your handwriting. Never could."

He faced Charlie, his stare and his tension strong enough to break glasses and false teeth. "The hell with it." He snatched the copy paper to crumple it.

Charlie stopped him. "I'll try harder." He reclaimed the copy paper. "First I want to read your mind."

"Charlie, I don't want to talk."

"How about listening to me?"

"Get to work."

"Don't hand me an assignment I can't fill."

"You're back on the payroll."

"I quit."

"Could be a funny column."

"Could be. If I had a mind to put to it. Which I don't."

"The hell with it. I've got a half-dozen columns in type."

"I like the Zero Mostel idea."

"Then shut up and write it."

Charlie shut up and the four jet engines roared for him and took their roar from the runway to a pattern in a sky not meant for patterns. Devers looked out the window and sought the horizon to the south.

And then he heard Charlie again. "Dev?" He faced him. "Forgive me. It's that kind of a day. I woke up so damn happy, so damn alive, so damn stupid. Dev, what's happened?"

"The happening's tonight in—"

"Where's Mag?"

"Mag's fine."

"Where is she?"

"She's at the wheel."

"Headed where?"

Devers told him.

Charlie turned green. "Not Mag. She won't drive into Manhattan. What happened? Herbert?"

"Letty Hines."

"Jesus! Well, that explains San Francisco."

Devers said nothing.

"What are you going to tell Miles?"

"Nothing."

Charlie hesitated. "I get it."

"Get to work."

"You expect Miles to tell you how to kill the boy—"

"Charlie, shut up."

"I know what Miles is going to tell you. Want to hear it?"

"From Miles."

"I can tell you more than Miles can."

"Don't, Charlie."

"The boy in you *is* dead."

Devers brought a cigarette to his sealed lips, but he did not light it. The warning signs about seat belts and smoking were on.

Charlie went on. "The boy in me *was* dead. Boys are like cats with nine lives. You made the boy in me live again. I'm not saying I can do the same for you. But I'll be around so you can see that it's so. So you can believe it can happen to you."

"I don't want it to happen."

"Why must only the bad happen? Shall I tell you about the bad? Shall I tell you what it means to be over sixty, over the hill, over your wife's dead body, over your dead newspaper?"

"I know, Charlie."

"The hell you do. Let me tell you about shame. About depravity. About degeneracy."

"Shut up, Charlie."

"The sooner I tell you, the sooner I get to Zero Mostel and Don Drysdale."

"And where do I get to?"

"You get to being scared."

The warning lights were off. Other warning lights burned in Charlie's eyes. "Of what?"

"Of slipping away. Of slipping into the bottle. Of slipping into slime and drowning in it."

"It's all behind you now."

"I know. And it's ahead of you."

"You and your crystal ball."

"How old is Letty Hines?"

"Forget her."

Devers turned to the window and looked in vain to see if God had plucked Letty Hines from friendly skies. He did continue to hear Charlie. And Charlie was not friendly.

"Look at me when I talk to you." Devers faced him. "My eyes might tell you something my shame might censor."

"They tell me enough."

Charlie told him more.

"Enough, Charlie."

Charlie told him too much.

Devers searched for a stewardess. He wanted his whiskey now.

"Dev, remember you used to sing in the shower?"

"I remember."

"In the black period that ended last Saturday—when you sat me down at the typewriter—I used to come up out of the slime into the shower and I'd scream and pray the neighbors'd mistake it for singing."

"I know what you mean," said Devers.

"No, you don't. You haven't learned how to scream yet. But you will."

"Are you going to teach me?"

"If you'd let me, I'd teach you many things."

"Such as?"

"Miles can't save you."

"If he can't—"

"Damn it, you're saved!" Charlie lowered his voice. "You're safe, I'm safe now, we're all safe with Scripps-Howard. And you'd better believe it."

"I can't."

"If Miles tells you so, will you believe it then?"

"Yeah."

"You're sure he won't, aren't you?"

"Yeah."

"If he tells you to jump off the Golden Gate—?"

"I never jump off bridges." Devers was with Mag in Virginia when he said, "Bridges aren't made for jumping. Only for crossing from nightmares to dreams."

"Thank you, Mister Verrazano. That was beautiful. But it hardly explains why high-diving is a major sport in San Francisco. Or why the sins of children must be visited upon their fathers."

"The sins of children? Have you got that right?"

"I'm afraid so. Jesus, I'm afraid."

FOUR

Beyond the arrival gate, in the swarm of faces, Devers sought his son and saw him not. He was betraying his bewilderment and disappointment to Charlie when he heard a nearby soprano voice calling his name.

A long-legged girl in a Misty Harbor raincoat rushed to him and embraced him. Shelley Anne Post, bright and comely. She embraced Charlie and told him how happy she and Miles were for him before she turned and made Devers sad.

Miles sent his regrets, Miles sent his girl, Miles was in Berkeley. In conference with a visiting mathematician. Miles will explain.

Shelley thought it would be fitting for the three of them to hasten to the nearest bar and click glasses, join souls, and touch knees under the table. Charlie was willing, Devers was not. Charlie argued, lost, and left for Los Angeles. Devers telephoned the Mark Hopkins. He was staying in San Francisco until he saw Miles.

When Shelley entered the taxi, Devers noted that she was wearing ballet slippers, blue Danskin leotards, a tartan miniskirt, and that her grace did not extend to her ankles. He sat still as she clutched his hands, and tried her soap-and-water smile.

"How's Miles?" he asked.

"Hateful. I hate him because I love him so ridiculously much. But I fell in love with you at first sight, and I don't think I'm ever going to hate you, and I want you to love me much too much because you're to be one of my children's two grandfathers."

"In or out of wedlock?"

She laughed and Devers forwarded her laughter to Ring Lardner. "Oh, you're marvelous. And, no, Milo hasn't proposed to me. Not once. I propose to him every time I crawl into bed with him, but he says no, and I can't say no to him. And so I just go on popping the pill every day and—" She broke off to pose a question. "Do you believe in the pill?"

"I'll believe whatever you tell me about it."

She laughed and kicked her feet high. "Oh, I love you. You're so much nicer than Milo. No comparison. He's a pale imitation—a pale copy of the original. Not only does he resist my connubial yearnings, but he resists cleverness, and I do so love clever men."

He was not lying when he said, "You're clever, too."

"Well, thank you. My dear damned parents would be delighted to hear you say so."

"I'll give you a note you can take home with you."

She found a blue Kleenex in her coat pocket, brought it to her nose, and blew hard. "I have a cold. Not *that* kind of a cold." She laughed. "My mother is Mrs. Newton Dunning of the Baltimore Dunnings. I do hope you're as unimpressed as I am."

He said nothing. He was thinking about Charlie.

"About my hair. Do you think it's cut too short?"

"I agree with Miles."

"Milo doesn't approve and he's a son of a bitch when he doesn't approve. Do you know why I cut my hair short?"

"Does Miles know?"

The fingers of her right hand were in the flesh of his left arm. "He knows everything and he knows nothing. I cut my hair short not so that I might be mistaken for a boy or for a dyke, but because I fervently believe that ears—if they wish to hear—if they yearn to hear all that's being said—must be exposed—must be free to catch all the words without which the music is of no import. Do you follow me?"

"I'm impressed by Radcliffe."

"Milo isn't. The son of a bitch."

"What does Miles see in you?"

"When did you stop calling him Milo? When he went to Harvard?"

"Possibly."

"Harvard impress you?"

"Yeah."

"Because you say 'yeah' instead of 'yes'?"

"I'm from Brooklyn," he said.

"That must've been ages and ages ago. Brooklyn is where the queers go to live when they weary of Third Avenue."

"You were telling me about Miles."

"I hadn't begun to tell you about Milo." She moved closer to him. "What do you think about me so far?"

"What does Miles think about you?"

"You are clever, and my how you do put me down. Like son, like father. There's only one thing that troubles me about you. Your cleverness doesn't seem to pleasure you. True or false?"

He understood her and the understanding dismayed him. "What did you major in at Radcliffe?"

"Obnoxiousness, excellent sir."

"*Summa cum laude,* no doubt."

She allowed him to see the talons of short, unpolished fingernails before she assaulted his left ear. "Fuck you, excellent sir."

Devers heard Shelley. He saw Mag on the floor of the closet. He heard Mag. He saw the gang-fuckers.

FIVE

The taxi left the freeway for the streets, billboards, banners, and bullhorns. Vote Kennedy. Vote McCarthy.

Devers brought lamentations instead of hurrahs to the city no longer alive or beautiful to him.

He banished the cable cars to Disneyland. He deeded Union Square to the pigeons. He bulldozed Nob Hill, and he welcomed the sight of the Mark Hopkins only because it would put walls beyond walls between Miles' girl and him.

The taxi stopped. Devers turned to Shelley. "Where would you like to be dropped off?"

"I'm with you, sir."

She was, and he could not lose her. She chatted with the bellhop and heard him declare for Kennedy. She heard the elevator operator declare for McCarthy, and she refereed the debate.

Devers the sleep-runner studied the geography of the eleventh-floor room: twin beds separated by a night table and a telephone, two windows, a writing desk and chair, an upholstered chair, a reading lamp, a television set, a bureau, a radiator, a closet, a bathroom. And a bottle of Jack Daniel's and fixings, compliments of the management.

He tipped the bellhop, who lingered to hear Shelley's lecture on the two-party system.

The lecture over, the bellhop gone, Shelley flopped down on the bed nearer to the door and shut her eyes.

"I'm safe now," said Devers. "You can go."

"I'll have a drink. Lying down."

"You keep saying anything but goodbye."

She put the telephone to her left ear. To Devers she said, "My mission, excellent sir, is not yet accomplished." She gave the operator a number. "Your darling son specifically instructed me to remain by your side until you depart from our fair city."

He deferred his parting shot because she was on the telephone and because Jack Daniel was calling him.

"Just over ice for me, thank you."

He fixed one drink, took it to the window, and was fixing his concern on Mag when he heard Shelley leave a message for Miles to call his father at the Mark.

Shelley left the bed for the bottle.

"Thanks and goodbye," said Devers.

"Did you like Bogie?"

He said nothing.

She spoke of Bogie, Toots Shor, and Jack Daniel's. She went on about *The Maltese Falcon,* the Brattle Theater, and asked him if it was true that Bogie had called him nothing but a fucking disappointed ball player.

He did not answer.

"Look, you fucking disappointed father! I can't leave you! I have my orders. I dislike—I intensely dislike—taking orders from anyone! But Milo—dear Lord of Love—isn't just anyone!"

Because he felt nothing, he said nothing. He watched her empty her glass and leave the bed. He thought he was rid of her when she set her glass down, but he was not. She removed her coat, flung it across a bed, and took the door that led to the bathroom.

Devers had another drink and another thought about Mag.

It was two o'clock in San Francisco, and it was five o'clock wherever Mag was. She was twelve and a half hours out of Valley Stream, out of Donna's closet, out of Nancy Glaviano's basement.

Shelley emerged from the bathroom. Strangely contrite, strangely humble. "I flushed the horrid Cliffie down the toilet. I'm upset. I had a row with Miles last night. May I tell you about it?"

He wanted to hear about Miles. He listened to her crack an ice cube with her good teeth. He watched her lie down on the bed close to the windows and exercise her legs.

"I am—I was—on an astrology kick. I am—I was—looking for law and order in the cosmos. Looking for God, whom I once presumed to be dead. In the past month, without telling Milo, I've devoured scores of books on the subject. Nevertheless, last night—in bed—I broached the matter of astrology. Your dear, darling son impolitely and brashly told me to shut my stupid mouth and go to sleep. I talked, I shouted. But, do you know this about your lousy son? You may elicit comments from him, but never passion. He told me that if the ten most brilliant brains in the world were brought together and asked to name the ultimate in man's stupidity they would—without question—without dissent—name the nonsense that calls itself astrology."

She gasped and pounded her free hand across her breasts as she was choked and chilled by a sliver of ice. "There are two things I cannot abide: the superiority of men, the inferiority of women. I promptly left his inadequate bed, called a cab, dressed, and departed. This morning my telephone rang. Milo calling. No apology, no regrets. Merely a command from my lord and liege. Get thee to the airport, wench. I'm a charwoman sweeping the universe of Milo Devers." She rattled the ice in her glass. "I'm a bum. I follow a bastard from

Cambridge. And he's such a bastard when he's mad, and he's good and mad about the prick who married your beautiful daughter."

"Miles is wrong."

"You dirty old apostate! Is the world flat?"

"More so every day."

"I loathed Herbert in Cambridge, I loathed him in—"

"Goodbye."

"I can't leave!"

She took one of the two San Francisco newspapers. "I'll be as quiet as a mouse and I'll study my horoscope. Please, sir, I have my orders."

He kept his silence, she kept her silence. She read her newspaper on her bed, he read his newspaper on his bed. He put the newspaper away when he read a headline about a head-on collision that had taken four lives somewhere south of San Francisco.

"May I talk to you about your mother?"

"No."

"Did she find God through Catholicism?"

"She was looking for a miracle for my sister."

"Nothing for herself?"

"She had sweet America. That was her miracle."

"Where is sweet America?"

Devers shut up. He was not about to debate her.

"Where is the enemy?"

Silence.

"You can't have forgotten. You're Mister Memory."

Patience.

"You and I, we're like the two tramps waiting for Godot."

Indifference.

"Who bit your hand?"

"My dog."

"You haven't got a dog. Your wife didn't want another dog after your first dog died."

"You're miscast as Mister Memory."

She persisted. "Did your wife bite your hand?"

"Yeah."

"Why?"

"It's the hand that feeds her."

"You're one of those un-American bastards who doesn't keep firearms at home. That, of course, precludes the possibility that you shot your wife."

Devers lit a cigarette.

"Miles smokes cigars in bed."

"Maybe he's trying to tell you something."

"Let me tell you something. I have a psi trait. Extrasensory perception. ESP. I have the gift. I see your wife buried in your garden. I see it in your eyes. I saw it in Charlie's eyes."

"What does your headshrinker say about this?"

"Your son is the messenger of evil. He'll destroy the last vestige of your soul."

"What soul?"

"The soul, bewildered sir, is the body's ability to say 'nonetheless.' "

"Is there a fate worse than you?"

"Abandon your cleverness, sir. It's a language that abuses Milo the Nolan."

"Milo the who?"

"Milo the Nolan. So called after Bruno—Giordano Bruno—the Italian philosopher, who was burned as a heretic. I suggest that, inasmuch as you are Irish, you speak Irish. Synge, sir, put the question: 'What is the price of a thousand horses against a son when there is one son only?' Care to comment, sir?"

"No," he said, listening to Mag scream at Donna to get off the telephone and into Radcliffe.

"Sir, be more afraid of your son than the sea."

Devers was at Debden with a pilot whose P-47 Thunderbolt had plunged into the English Channel.

"Are you Aries, Taurus, Gemini—?"

"I'm sleepy." He shut his eyes.

"Sleep on the plane."

"What plane?"

"To Los Angeles and out of danger."

"Shut the door on your way out."

"Milo ordered me not—"

"Goodbye, Miss Post." He was on his feet, gathering her raincoat and holding it for her.

She did not stir. "I'll be as still as a mouse."

He flung the coat at her. "Goodbye."

"I'll read in the bathtub."

"Goodbye."

Recognizing wrath, she turned away and exited. He shut the door, he locked it, and he tried to put her out of his mind. He was back in Debden, drinking to the dead of the 4th Fighter Group, when he heard a rapping on the door.

He opened it and saw Shelley. She begged permission to make one urgent telephone call. He relented.

Soon she was speaking to a Jerome Grass, but he heard nothing beyond the name. The call ended, she turned to Devers. "Would you care to know what that was all about?"

"No."

"Well, back to my post. I'll be sitting outside the door."

He was thinking of house detectives, of Mag Griffin and Carleton Dabney, when he ordered Shelley to sit down and be quiet. He was going to sleep.

Eyes shut, Devers heard the sea. He remembered hearing the sea two hundred miles inland: the sound of a cotton mill at night. He remembered hearing the sea on a road through a pine woods sound like a steam locomotive. He remembered the low country girl drinking Green River whiskey, hearing the unseen train, grabbing the wheel of the Model-A Ford at a crossing. He remembered the overturned car in the ditch, the screams to Jesus, the thanks to Jesus. Easter in South Carolina, 1937.

Devers understood that the low country girl and Shelley Anne Post were not sisters except under the skin of their forebodings. It was not Miles he had to beware, it was Miles' girl.

SIX

The first ring woke Devers. When he turned to reach for the telephone, he saw that Shelley was napping in the other bed.

It was Charlie Spencer and he wanted to kiss Walter O'Malley.

"Make sure he removes his cigar."

Charlie appreciated the humor, but not the tenor of it. "You haven't seen Miles."

"No."

"You alone?"

"No."

"Shelley?"

"Yeah."

"Another Letty Hines?"

"No."

"Don't, huh?"

"No, Charlie."

"You can still make it to the ball park."

"Charlie, I wouldn't have it any other way. And I'm with you, you know that."

"You're not with me. If you were, you'd be into the Wild Turkey."

"Have one for me."

"The bottle stays shut until about midnight tonight. If there are no extra innings, and I know you're all right."

"I'm all right, Charlie."

"You don't sound it."

"Bad connection."

"You sure?"

"Look out for Drysdale."

"You look out for curves. Not Shelley's, but the kind Miles can throw you."

"I got the message, Charlie."

When he replaced the telephone, Devers saw that Shelley was awake and staring at him.

"Mr. Spencer?"

"The house detective."

"You're dreaming."

"Do you believe in dreams?"

"I will. When Milo marries me."

"Miles your first love?"

"Yes. If you discount a girl from Sarah Lawrence."

He said nothing.

"Milo knows. Milo knows all. But, you, sir, does that queer me with you?"

He left his bed, went to a window, and wondered how fresh the air would be if he went out and down, down and out.

The telephone again.

No sweetness, no innocence. "Hello." All brightness. "Milo, my love!" Laughter. "Dear Daddy'll be with you in a minute. He's zipping his fly."

Devers took the slander and the telephone. He listened to Miles apologize for being detained in Berkeley. A problem in topology, a promise he had made, an appointment he had to keep. Could Devers remain in San Francisco for dinner? He could, he suggested the Blue Fox. Miles had a counter-suggestion. Lee Wu's. Seven o'clock. And then he asked Devers to put Shelley on.

Shelley, happy to be on again, listened, pouted, bit her lips, and found rage before she slammed down the telephone.

It was 3:50 P.M. and Devers was counting the hours when he heard Shelley. "How about a matinee?"

He played dumb. The view from the window was beautiful. He could see all the way to seven o'clock.

"Excellent sir, let me take you to the flicks?"

"What's playing?"

"*Triangle 3* and *Emma, C'est Moi.*"

"Never heard of them."

"Underground flicks."

"Stag reels."

"*Ars gratia artis.*"

"Beautiful arse, no doubt."

"I play Emma Bovary."

"Perfect casting."

"Aren't you at all interested in seeing what your bastard son has no interest in seeing?"

"If it's not good enough for Miles—"

"Fuck Miles, fuck your cleverness." As she reached for her raincoat, she began to weep. At the door she turned to him. "I can't make you understand, I can't make you afraid of Miles."

SEVEN

Seven o'clock. No Miles.

Devers saw that his son had been there. On the table, with the tea and cups, were a copy pencil and sheets of copy paper flecked by algebra.

As he waited, Devers lit a cigarette and blew smoke at Lee Wu's orange dragons until he heard someone at the curtains. He turned, his stomach turned.

"Hello, Dad."

The shape and substance were right. The tenor, the eyes, and the beard were wrong.

Devers' smile was right. "Hello, Miles."

Miles sat and looked cross. "I've got a cold."

"Does it hurt you when you smile?"

"I'm sorry." Miles gathered pencil and paper.

"Finish it."

"There's no finish. The problem remains."

"Bad day at Berkeley?"

"Very." Miles poured tea for Devers and himself.

"Losing your fascination with math?"

"No, with *Ramparts.* I'm leaving at the end of the month."

The news stunned Devers. "Where do you go from here?"

"Princeton," said the condemned man bound for San Quentin.

"*Princeton,*" Devers said, reading the geography of his dreams.

"Institute for Advanced Study. Two-year appointment."

The waiter brought the soup. Miles took his spoon.

Devers did not. "Then why was it a bad day at Berkeley?"

Miles ate a won ton and coughed. "Two reasons. Your telegram. Your telephone message."

"Nothing else?"

Miles took and examined Devers' bitten hand. "Did Mom do this?"

"You talked to Shelley."

"Just got off the phone. She called me."

"It's all right. I buried your mother deep enough."

"I didn't believe her."

"I could bury your mother in your beard."

"Where's Mom?"

Crushing his cigarette, Devers told his son about the note on the kitchen table, the missing suitcases and station wagon.

"What happened?"

"Let your mother tell you. If she can."

"I'm asking you."

"When we get back to the hotel, you can place a call to Columbia. Aunt Catherine may know what hotel, hospital, or morgue—"

"I'll make the call here." Miles explained that Lee Wu's son James was a Harvard friend. "Have your soup."

"If it were chicken soup, it wouldn't help me."

Miles found compassion. "What would?"

"An answer from you."

"Dad, I can give you questions, quotations. But no answers."

"Did Shelley warn you about giving me answers?"

Miles frowned. "She told me she warned you about me."

"Should I take the warning?"

Miles spooned soup.

"Was Shelley right to warn me?"

More soup. "She has the right."

"You gave Donna an answer."

"The riddle?"

"The two black pebbles."

Miles chewed a won ton. "I told Donna how *she* might find the answer."

Devers was sharp. "It was the answer itself. You know it was."

Miles read the won tons in the bowl. "I gave her Herbert. Had I known—"

"I like Herbert."

Miles read Devers. "Good."

"I like Donna again."

"Good."

"You're humoring me."

Miles struck the bowl with his spoon. "Dad! What the hell do you think I want to hear? Herbert and Donna are good news from you! Good! Great! Mom is fucking bad news!"

Devers looked for bourbon in his bowl. "Would you give your mother an answer?"

"To what?"

"Hamlet's question."

"Fuck Hamlet! Did Mom try—?"

"Yeah."

"She failed."

"Who says she failed?"

"You saved her."

"Who says she's saved? Make the call. Save her."

Miles spooned agony. "Have you given up, Dad?"

"Yeah. I tried. I thought I had an answer to give your mother. I gave it to her. I have nothing more to give her. You. Anyone. I came to you for the answers. To save your mother. And myself."

Miles was bitter. "Hamlet's question?"

"Please. Make the call."

The boy who had asked for a clock on his fifth birthday checked his wristwatch. "Eighteen hours. Seven hundred miles. Mom could be in Columbia."

Devers shook his head. "No chance. Fifty miles is her distance record. Behind the wheel. When she was well."

"Did you make any calls?"

"Three. This afternoon when I was alone. New York, Washington, Richmond. United Press International had no report on any highway fatality involving Mrs. Forrest Devers."

"You look hung-over, Dad."

"I had my last drink before I made the first call."

"There's a bottle of Canadian Club in Lee Wu's desk."

"Bring me a bottle with a message in it."

EIGHT

Devers was alone. He took no tea, no food. He smoked one cigarette after another, pushed one minute after another, and took on one terror after another.

Seventy-one minutes later Miles returned. Devers looked and saw no beard. He saw 1957, a boy struck dead. *Delenda est Brooklyn.* Brooklyn must be destroyed. O'Malley.

Miles sat down. "Richmond. The Jefferson."

"Alive?"

"Distraught."

"What floor?"

"Does it matter?"

"No," said Devers. "A chair is high enough."

"Mom can't stand up. She's dizzy, her head's splitting. The strain of driving."

"When she's able to stand up, what then?"

"She hopes to leave at daybreak."

"For Columbia?"

"Yes."

"Did she call Catherine?"

"They were on the phone for over an hour."

"What did Catherine tell you?"

"I didn't let her tell me anything but where Mom is."

"What did your mother tell you?"

"What did she tell me or what did I hear?"

"What did she tell you?"

"Too much."

"And what did you hear?"

"Enough."

"Enough to solve all riddles?"

"No."

"No understanding?"

"Some."

The waiter appeared with hot food. Miles served himself.

"Didn't spoil your appetite," said Devers.

"Feed a cold, Grandma Devers used to say."

"Did your mother tell you about Grandma Griffin and me?"

Food in his mouth, Miles nodded. Devers waited for him to speak, but Miles did nothing but eat.

"One thing about Chinese food, an hour later you're starved for emotion."

Miles smiled. "Good. I'm hungry for humor."

"No comment about Grandma Griffin and me?"

"The act itself? Or the act of confessing it?"

"Both."

"Were you seduced?"

"Didn't your mother tell you that?"

"No. She told me you confessed to having an affair with her mother."

"Did you believe that?"

Miles met Devers' stare. "I'll believe what you tell me."

Devers talked, Miles ate. When Devers was done, he had to wait for his son's reaction.

Miles said, "Another Miles, another time. I'm there and not there. Dead and unborn."

Devers said nothing. He waited to hear more.

"Why Letty?"

"What did your mother tell you?"

"She cried incest. Again. Letty for Donna. Mom kept repeating what you told her about sleeping with your mother, your sister—"

"Hold it!" He told Miles what he had said to Mag.

Miles heard and understood. "You forgot one thing."

"Freud? Sophocles? Sophomorism?"

Miles poured tea for Devers and for himself. "The most important thing your father ever told you."

Devers found his father's voice. " 'Be careful what you tell people, they may not always understand you.' "

"Right."

"Pop never instructed me how to raise the dead."

"No." Miles was distant. Devers waited for him to return. "Know where I am?"

"Richmond."

"Wurtsboro Hill," said Miles.

"It's gone."

"Grandpa Devers. The Westcott. The Wurtsboro Hill. The Water Man. The way from Brooklyn to Princeton."

"When did Pop tell you this?"

"The day Harvard accepted me. We talked on the phone."

"Did you understand him?"

Miles nodded from his distance. "The Westcott, grandpa's first car. Bought second-hand from Vanbroeck, who had taken it from a bankrupt debtor. A lemon of a motor car. Unable to take the Wurtsboro Hill in high. Or in second without having to buy sweetwater from the Water Man for the steaming radiator. Dollar a bucket. Grandpa believed if the Westcott could just once make the hill in high, without stopping for water, his and your dreams would come true. Vanbroeck's promises would be fulfilled. Grandpa would inherit Vanbroeck's Bush Terminal plant. And you'd make it to Princeton."

"Sweet America," Devers lamented. "Route 17 was the summer way to Liberty, where my mother and sick sister looked for four-leaf clovers. The Wurtsboro Hill was God's little mountain. To my father the Water Man was Fate. Oh, the money we burned on special oils, special spark plugs, special tuneups, and what not."

"A waste," said Miles.

"Like all American dreams?"

"American follies."

"The folly that's taking you to Princeton."

"Not by Route 17."

"Did you mock Pop when he—?"

"I love grandpa."

"Love or loved?"

"I love him. He lives in you, he lives in me."

"Route 17 lives."

"It never led to four-leaf clovers."

"Neither did Lourdes. As Pop used to complain."

Miles hesitated. "Grandpa believed."

"In the American Dream."

"In God."

"Whose God? Are you one of those revisionists rewriting

history? He was *my* father. I know who and what he was. He spit on the church. He spit on the crucifix in Karen's room. Sure he believed in God. He believed in Emrich Vanbroeck."

"Vanbroeck was dead."

"The hell you say. In death Vanbroeck was still Pop's God. Pop never blamed him, never cursed him for forsaking—"

"Vanbroeck was a prick."

Devers looked for his son and saw nothing but the beard. "Why? Because he dropped dead?"

"Because he hired grandpa's dream. The renegade Irishman always sober, always at the office. Eight days a week. And one big lie to keep him going. It will someday all be yours."

"Only the Bush Terminal plant. Not the sash factory in Connecticut, not the glass works—"

"Nevertheless, Vanbroeck lied."

"He died before—"

"Dad!"

Devers did not desist. "Pop blamed Vanbroeck's lawyer."

"Arthur Sevilla."

"Pop tell you—?"

"Arthur Sevilla told me."

Devers saw mazes in the beard. "He died two years ago. He was eighty-seven. How did you get to Arthur Sevilla? Route 17?"

Miles grinned. He reached into a pocket and found a panatela. "Harvard." He lit the cigar with Devers' matches. "Sevilla's grandson, Dick Rack, was a classmate. Arthur Sevilla asked Dick if I was related to Thomas Aquinas Devers."

"You never told me."

"In ancient times those who brought bad news to the king brought death to themselves."

"What bad news? What could be worse than what happened in 1933?"

"It was so bad I never told grandpa. I let him die blaming Jew lawyers and—"

"What did Sevilla tell you?"

"He remembered you. I reminded him of you."

"Get to Pop!"

"Vanbroeck always intended to leave everything to Princeton."

"Get to Pop!"

Miles said, "I quote Sevilla quoting Vanbroeck: 'Tom's a good lieutenant, but there's no larceny in his heart. He'd never make anything but a good lieutenant.'"

"Ah, Christ!"

"Sevilla agreed with Vanbroeck."

"Did you agree with Sevilla?"

"I did."

"Anything else?"

"Sevilla recalled nothing about Vanbroeck's promise to get you into Princeton. He believed Vanbroeck would have kept his promise had he lived. He knew Vanbroeck was unable to think of himself as dead—and you alive in Princeton."

"Sweet Vanbroeck."

"The property of Devers & Son in Bay Ridge belonged to Princeton."

"The rent checks were mailed to Sevilla." Devers laughed. "There I was in Bay Ridge dreaming of lost Princeton and I was on Princeton ground—did Sevilla know about my Pulitzer?"

"Not until I told him. He was impressed."

"Are you still impressed?"

"I haven't finished about grandpa."

"More from Sevilla?"

"From grandpa himself. In 1943—during the war—he muffed what he called his second chance."

"Second chance at what?"

"His American Dream. His American number. His million."

"What the hell are you smoking? 1943? Pop was grossing about a hundred thousand, netting maybe ten."

Miles contined to smoke. "Remember this name? *Alan Burnside.*"

Devers remembered. "Commission broker. Broad Street, Manhattan. Lumber products."

"In 1943," said Miles, "Burnside presented a war priority affidavit for grandpa's signature."

"I knew that. Pop didn't sign it. He didn't sign it because it was a lie. He was doing no war work."

"It wasn't the lie that stopped him."

"A lie always stopped Pop! *Larceny* stopped him. If you paid for sugar pine, you got sugar pine. Christ, to Pop a knot in a sash rail was a lie!"

Miles drew on the cigar. He blew smoke at an orange dragon before he faced Devers. "I quote grandpa: '*What if God saw me and gave my boy back to me in a pine box?*' "

The saws were ripping him, the sawdust burying him, the sugar pine scent choking him. Devers could not shout, cry out, or make a human sound.

NINE

There was a misery of minutes before Devers was able to raise his head, his eyes, and his voice.

"When did you hear this?"

"1960. You were in Pittsburgh. The Series."

"Was Pop drunk?"

"Drinking."

"Was he bitter?"

"Wistful. We were playing the McCormack records."

"Mourning his sweet Miriam?"

"Grandma's name wasn't mentioned. He spoke of Vanbroeck. The Jews who owned the Bush Terminal plant. And Father Coughlin."

"That son of a bitch, he made millions. Not Pop in his church. Never missed a Sunday morning. Reading his Sunday *Times.* Checking his books, his machines, his sugar pine, and dreaming of a Monday when the telephone'd never stop ringing with orders. Because all of a sudden quality and workmanship and pride and honesty would stand for something in sweet America. No, Pop never sold a bad pair of sash, never broke a promise, always broke his ass, his heart, and never made his million."

"Grandpa believed he might have—had you stayed with him."

"Give me the quote."

" 'Something happened between Forrest and me.' "

"Vanbroeck happened."

"Grandpa didn't say. You tell me."

Devers took Miles to 1933, to Flatbush, to the garage, to the Buick.

Miles was moved. "He never told me."

"Maybe Pop was afraid you wouldn't understand."

"I think he wanted me to understand that he wasn't about to damn his son before your son as his son had damned him."

"You lost me."

"Must be the influence of Joyce. 'Who is the father of any son that any son should love him or he any son?' "

"Good question, good Joyce."

"If grandpa was trying to kill himself—"

"You doubt me?"

"What was the motive? The insurance money?"

"No. No insurance, no sacrifice. Shame. Escape."

"What was the shame?"

Devers frowned. "He was forsaken. He was a fool. A failure."

"He had to fail," said Miles.

Devers wanted to damn his son, but he deferred his wrath. "Why?"

"Sweet America."

"What about sweet America?"

"It was a myth. A never-never land."

"Who the hell are you quoting now?"

"Myself."

"Then damn you and your fucking Harvard ignorance."

Miles did not relent. "The real America belonged to the Vanbroecks. The real estate, the real money, the real power. The Vanbroecks invest their money. What did grandpa invest but his heart and soul? On what exchange was grandpa's investment listed? Whose lists? Frank Merriwell? Horatio Alger? What was sweet about America to the Vanbroecks was the pot. The kitty. The fortune that's the sum of misfortune, corruption, and the kind of patriotism now having a nervous breakdown."

Devers said, "Taking your soap box to Princeton?"

"It's not Vanbroeck's Princeton I'm going to. Not in Vanbroeck's Westcott by way of Wurtsboro Hill. Not in Vanbroeck's Buick by way of carbon monoxide."

"Remember to change trains at Princeton Junction."

"I'll remember. That's what America ought to be about. Change, chance, and challenge."

"What soured you on *Ramparts?*"

Miles considered the question. "No end justifies the means.

The means are all. If America is to be sweet, the means must be sweet."

"Are you affirming the American Dream?"

"Not from a soap box. From the moon. Looking off into space and discovering the blue planet. The blue dream."

Devers liked what he heard. "I take back what I said about Harvard ignorance."

"Harvard confusion."

"Miles?"

"Yes, Dad?"

"Did you give your mother an answer?"

"Mom had her answer. You gave it to her."

"Will you give me my answer?"

"If I can, I'll lead you to find it for yourself. What's the question?"

"How do I kill the boy hiding within me before he kills me?"

Miles coughed, fell silent, put the cigar away, and gave his attention. "Dad, are you a wise man?"

"No. Make me wise."

"If you were a wise man, I could reproach you."

"Reproach isn't what—"

"It's part of the answer."

"I'm not above reproach."

"Quotes are also part of the answer. 'Reprove a wise man and he will love you.' Do you buy that?"

"I do."

"Do you buy this? Your son at five is your master. At ten your slave. At fifteen your double. After that, your friend or foe—depending upon your son's upbringing."

"Sounds wise," said Devers.

"Oriental wisdom. Why must you kill the boy in you?"

"The boy refuses to accept the death of things. Kennedy. The *World-Telegram.* The *World Journal Tribune.* The boy prevents me from becoming what I should be. A man among men. A *mensch*."

"Name one *mensch*."

"Einstein."

Miles said nothing.

"Foolish choice. I don't guess geniuses—"

"Foolish choice," Miles agreed. "Einstein never killed the boy hiding within him."

"I don't believe it."

"Any other name—?"

"Let's stay with Einstein. You made a statement. Prove it."

"Einstein died believing that God does not play at dice." Miles went on about the unified field theory, the attempt to solve the riddle of the universe. "The point is this: the *menschen* of science believe Einstein was wrong to pursue this theory. But he did pursue it in the face of criticism, abuse, and lamentation. He gave to it what he had given to his two relativity theories and the other discoveries made when he was in the country of the young. Do you understand, Dad?"

"Einstein or you?"

"Neither of us. The boy hiding within you."

Devers hesitated. "Are you a *mensch* or still a boy?"

"A *mensch* is a myth. An ideal. I'm a boy."

"Where is this country of the young? Vietnam? When I get to Cleveland tomorrow shall I ask Buchanan to send me there to cover the war?"

"It's fully covered, Dad. With enough American shame."

"Shall I apply for a job at *Ramparts?*"

Miles ignored the absurd.

"Shall I quit and write my Civil War book?"

"Grant and Buckner?"

"Yeah."

"Any other ideas for books?"

"One. This is the title. *How I Killed the Boy Hiding Within Me.*"

"Change the title. *How I Killed Frank Merriwell.*"

"Tell me more."

Miles stroked his beard. "Merriwell fumbles. Yale loses to Harvard. Merriwell, in the locker room, smiles in defeat. He's learned to lose games, wars, and everything but heart. He's learned that games aren't life, that wars aren't."

"What is?" Devers demanded.

"Life is. Say farewell to the myths that foul our compasses. Say, farewell, Frank Merriwell. Farewell, Jack Kennedy."

"Farewell, Camelot," said Devers.

"There was no Camelot. If there had been, Bobby would be McCarthy's lieutenant instead—"

"There was no Dallas."

"There is. Dallas was last seen in Memphis."

"How does Einstein explain that?"

Miles took tea.

Devers tried again. "How do you explain me?"

Miles said, "Let me quote a pessimist: 'We are basically something we should not be; thus it is normal that we one day will cease to exist.' "

Devers listened and waited to hear more.

"Quote an existentialist: 'Man is and must think of himself as a being-toward-death.' "

"I hate the boy in me."

"The only true dignity of man is his capacity to despise himself."

"I've got the capacity. June is busting out with capacity."

"Think laterally. Get your head out of the bag meant only for black pebbles. See the pebbled beach. See the answer before you. As clear as the blue earth seen from the moon."

Devers thought about the advice and saw nothing but blackness. "I can't get off the earth. I can't get away from sweet America. Merriwell. Camelot."

"Then you're in danger," said Miles. "Cling to what's close to you, to what you know, to what you can do. Cling to your friends, to your traditions, and to your love. Lest you be dissolved in a universal confusion and know nothing. And love nothing."

Devers clung to confusion. "You've contradicted yourself."

"I was also quoting J. Robert Oppenheimer."

"I need a drink."

" 'To get drunk alone or to lead a nation comes to the same thing.' Quote Sartre, who knows all about boys who hide within men. About boys who lie to themselves and try to persuade themselves they can abandon their boyhoods, leaving no forwarding address and losing the past to become someone unknown, yet someone who does things, who breathes the air of fresh, second winds."

"What the hell does a Frenchman like Sartre know about American boys?"

"Sartre understands the universality of man. He knows that unless things happen to a man and unless things die in a man that he'll never know what life is. Or was."

Devers stared at Miles, at eyes like black pebbles. "What's the good cheer from Camus?"

Miles hesitated. "Revolt."

"Against sweet America?"

"Against the condition of life."

"Like your mother did Sunday night?"

"Like you did Monday."

Bewildered, Devers said nothing.

"You gave Mom a challenge, a chance, a change. You gave her life."

"Then why is it wrong for me to revolt against the condition of my own life?"

"Mom had lost her function. You haven't."

"The savor is gone from the salt."

"Send the boy in you for fresh salt."

"To pour on my wounds?"

"No, it's too precious for—"

"Where will he find fresh salt?"

"Boston, Fenway Park. Frank Merriwell's back swinging a Polish sausage."

Devers had no quarrel with Miles' description of Carl Yastrzemski. "Where else? Brooklyn? Ebbets Field?"

"It's still there. The boy in you can find it. The same way he found Washington Park when it had vanished from Third Avenue. I know. You found it for me."

"How many cold ghosts can a grain of salt hold?"

"It's warm in Toots Shor's."

"No more. Gertrude Stein likes it cold."

" 'If the boy within you ceases to speak to you, then the shape of your life will surely be broken. And there remains nothing more to be said.' "

"Stein or Sartre?"

"Seán O'Faoláin."

"Up the Irish," said Devers without salt.

"It's simpler to renounce the things we've known than to surrender the things we've dreamed of."

"Shut up."

Miles did.

"Unless you've got a funny story."

"Let's take a walk."

"Where's the check?"

"No check."

"Thanks."

"Thank Lee Wu."

"I thought I was your guest."

"You won't thank me when you hear the story."

TEN

Devers minded the walk with Miles toward Union Square. It was not the chill in the night. In Miles. It was his feet. He felt as if he were walking in the weighted baseball spikes worn by Ty Cobb during spring training to strengthen his leg muscles.

Prompted by his father, Miles erred at once. He revealed the source of the story: a book owned by Shelley.

Devers frowned, said nothing, and listened.

"India. A village. A very narrow street. Darkness. The light of fires. A crowd gathers for a street show. The performers are a middle-aged magician and a very young, very small boy. The show begins. The magician tosses a forty-foot rope into the dark. It appears to be suspended vertically. Actually it's been caught by an unintroduced, unseen assistant, who hooks the rope to an unseen wire suspended between two buildings." Miles turned to Devers. "Are you with me?"

"Yeah."

"The magician—who wears a long, loose cloak—takes from it a long knife and a piece of fruit. He is peeling the fruit when the impish boy leaps, grabs the peeled fruit, and climbs the rope. To darkness. The magician, cursing the boy, brandishing the long knife, follows him up the rope. To darkness. The crowd sees nothing. It hears the boy screaming in peril, in agony, in torture. And then, out of the dark, the crowd sees and smells spilled blood crackling in the flames. One by one, bloody limbs drop into the fire. The crowd screams. Some faint, few flee. The fire roasts the limbs. And then down the rope comes the magician. Deftly he draws the crowd's attention to the collapsing of the rope. That done, he draws the crowd's attention to a covered wicker basket. The magician utters magic words, claps his hands. The cover flies from the basket, the boy leaps out. The act is over. The show is over."

Devers breathed the night air to chase his own nausea. "The story isn't."

"No," said Miles. "Another night, another town, another performance. One other difference: the magician has had too much hashish. But the show must go on. The routine begins. The rope. The fruit, the chase up the rope into darkness. The screams, the bloody limbs, everything as before. But the finish is different. The magician doesn't climb down the rope. He falls into the fire, a bloodied knife stuck into his heart."

"Where is the boy?" Devers asked.

"Dead. Dismembered. Roasting in the fire with the magician."

"What was in the wicker basket?"

"Emptiness."

"What went wrong?"

"The hashish made the magician forget one of the principals in his act: the freshly slaughtered monkey always conealed under his cloak, close to the harness that held and hid the boy."

Devers understood that he had been told a tale of a man who killed the boy hiding within him.

He fled from the roasting flesh, from Shelley, from Miles.

ELEVEN

Devers rushed into the first bar he passed. The bartender looked better to him than the blonde stripper in action. The Old Bushmills bottle looked best of all.

He was on his second shot when he sensed Miles' presence at the bar. Miles' silence was louder than the drums. The bartender read Devers' signal and poured a shot for Miles.

"I'm sorry, Dad."

Devers did not face his son. "Shall we drink to the slaughtered monkeys?"

"Shelley—"

"The hell with her. You deserve each other."

"No, we don't. She believes if you don't believe in life after death you're dead in this life that doesn't pass for life."

Devers faced Miles. "You're dead if you mention her name again. If you tell me another Indian—don't you know any funny Irish or Yiddish stories?"

Miles sipped his whiskey.

"The beard makes you look Jewish. Do you feel Jewish?"

"I did once. At Buchenwald."

"Not in Israel?"

"No."

"Did you feel Irish in Ireland?"

"Only in a cemetery in Cork."

"Do you feel American?"

"I did. In Ebbets Field."

"What will you feel in Princeton?"

"I'll feel my way."

"Toward Appomattox?"

"Confederate blood will tell."

Devers had another shot of Irish whiskey before he confronted Miles. "What did the two Confederates tell each other on the telephone tonight?"

"Dad, I listened to Mom."

"What did you hear?"

Miles hesitated. "Good news."

"Tell me. I'm starved for good news."

"Charlie. Donna. Herbert. Mom."

"Did you leave out Letty?"

"Letty."

"Good news?"

"Good news."

"Is that the way it looks from the moon?"

"From this bar stool."

Devers paid the bartender, slid off the stool, and left. Miles was right behind him.

Devers shook Miles' hand. "Goodbye."

"Where are you going?"

"Sorry I spoiled your day."

"Dad, where are you going?"

"You're going to work."

"Come along."

"I'm going back to the hotel."

"Have some dinner."

"I'll grab a sandwich, get to bed, and leave a two-o'clock call."

"Two o'clock in the morning?"

"Five o'clock in Richmond."

"Don't."

"Why not?"

"Think about it."

"Who doesn't want me to make the call? You or your mother?"

"Think about it."

Devers thought about it. "What happened to forever?"

"Tell yourself what you told grandpa when he put the question to you."

Devers was walking with his father away from his mother's grave when an unseen hand gripped his shoulder.

"Dad!"

Devers spun away from Miles. "Goodbye!"

Miles heard the agony and froze. Devers went on his way. At the corner of Powell and California, he stopped to survey the climb up Nob Hill. He made it in Ty Cobb's weighted spikes.

TWELVE

There were two long-distance telephone messages for Devers: call Dr. Teller in Valley Stream, call Mr. Spencer in Los Angeles. He made one call to room service for a Swiss cheese on white.

He sipped Jack Daniel's and partook of his sandwich in a Greek luncheonette in Bay Ridge, in communion with Jacob Wald.

Still drinking whiskey, he arose, went to the desk and

stroked the case of Jacob Wald's typewriter and felt the motion of the train carrying him south past Princeton Junction. To Richmond, to Columbia.

The past trailed him to the window. He raised it, observed a cable car clanging down California Street, and heard Hilda Chester ringing her cowbell in Ebbets Field. In Miles' America.

He drank while he undressed, he drank while he showered. He did not sing like John McCormack or scream like Charlie Spencer. He kept losing the bar of soap and kept trying not to lose the balance of his body, and of his mind.

Devers knew enough to sit down before getting into his pajamas. To position the straight chair before the unguarded window. To lie supine in the bed farther from the window.

In the dark he took Richmond.

Hello, Mag. I'm all alone. No telephone in hand, no whiskey in hand. I'm all alone by the telepathy. Miles said nothing about telepathy. Irving Berlin wrote nothing about it. Remember telepathy? Remember how when the kids were small you used to call me on the telephone at the *World-Telegram* and give me a list of things to pick up at the market on my way home? Remember how often there was something you needed, something you forgot to mention, and when it was too late to reach me by telephone you tried to reach me by mental telepathy? Remember how it sometimes worked, remember that when it did you'd smile and laugh and brag about your powers of telepathy?

Mag, I'm trying mine now. Are you alive? Awake? Caring? Listen, Mag, because there's more efficacy in listening than in prayers. For God's sake, Mag, let's bring our beds together and talk about abolishing the death of things.

Listen, Mag. God does not play at dice because Einstein and Miles forbid it. Miles sees Ebbets Field. He can't see Camelot. He hears you on the telephone and he can't see *us*.

You and me, Mag. The sum total of us, the beginning and the middle of us, the life of us, the love of us. He hears you and sees forever. The forever that begins in graves.

For God's sake, Mag, not forever. It's too soon. I see the cornsilk hair. I see the train. I see *us*.

Or do I? Do I remember it all as it never was? Think about it, Miles said. Key words from your son. Think. Remember. I think, I remember, I think I remember the way it was. I listen to Miles, and I come to know what I never knew and never would have known and never would have missed not knowing.

Excuse me, Mag. Telepathy doesn't make for the simple declarative. Telepathy doesn't make—

The news, Mag. Simple, declarative news. No emotion sickness. Miles is going to Princeton. By Route 17. Wurtsboro Hill. The Northwest Passage to Princeton discovered by Thomas Aquinas Devers. Miles has grown a beard. Did he tell you? No, he told you nothing. He told you everything by listening to you. And then, for an encore, he told me everything by not listening to me. Another key word from your bearded boy. Function. I have it. You don't.

Mag, I understand Miles about you. I don't understand him about me. Who the hell's been at my understanding? My ego? My pride? My vanity? My folly? What is it? I saw inside my father. Why can't Miles look and see what's inside of me? Under the skin of function. If he can see Ebbets Field, why can't he see me?

He's a bomb-thrower, the bearded one. What happened to his skates and his bikes and the *Playboy* under his bed? Bombs. Listen, Mag, listen to how he bombed me. Pop was convicted and doomed by Vanbroeck. The charge? No larceny. Pop paid a million-dollar ransom for my life. To whom? To the Lord God Jehovah.

Listen, listen to Miles, listen to him slaughter me like a monkey. A man who kills the boy hiding within himself ends by killing himself.

Indian story. A rope trick unknown to Nancy Glaviano. The book of Shelley. Miles has a cold. Shelley's cold. Or is it Miles' cold that—

Pop told Miles something. He said there was something between him and me. Pop and me. He never said what. I say it's a wall. I say send for O'Malley and his wrecking ball. I say it's a battleground. A killing ground. Once upon a time I was you, someday you'll be me. Someday it'll all be yours. All? Forever? Pass the baton, pass the whiskey, pass away. First, pass the secret. The warmest place in the world—

Ah, Mag. I'm drunk from drinking, spent from thinking. I've thought about it. It's simple as E = MC squared, as simple as HEE = HAW, as HO = HUM.

Be well, be glad to be alive, be without me. Be.

Devers heard a sound escaping from his open mouth. He could not tell whether it was a yawn or a groan.

Wednesday, June 5, 1968

ONE

Devers dreamed.

He was in Richmond, in Mag's bedroom at the Jefferson. Naked, he came to the bed and woke her. She opened her eyes to a stranger, she shut her eyes to fright. He spoke in a voice strange to himself, telling Mag he was Mister Memory. He promised marvel. Magic. Miracle. Open your eyes and I'll turn you into my sweetest memory of you. I can do it, Mag. I did it for America. America opened its eyes to me, and it's now sweet enough for clover to grow from the ashes in Dallas. Open your—

The telephone opened Devers' eyes in San Francisco. He faced the dark, the night table, the whiskey bottle, and the ringing telephone.

"Hello," he said to the vanished dream.

"Dad!"

He heard Miles as in a nightmare. A boy's horror before the breaking of his heart, the ending of his boyhood. 1957. *Delenda est Brooklyn.* Brooklyn must be destroyed. O'Malley. Oh, Christ.

"Kennedy's been shot!"

Devers banged the telephone down on 1963 and destroyed Dallas. He clutched for whiskey, emptied the bottle into his own emptiness, and flung it to the softness of the other bed before he fell back and waited for sleep to return him to Richmond.

The telephone rang for Camelot, for Dallas, for Arlington. Cradle and all, Devers flung it on the other bed.

The ringing gave way to frenzy and fury beyond the walls of the room.

Good God, what the hell's going on? Is he dead? They got him, they got him! He's been shot, he's been shot! Where the hell—? Los Angeles! Ambassador Hotel! My God, oh, my God! He's been shot, he's been shot! Jesus Christ! Oh, Jesus Christ, it can't be again! Not again! What's America coming to! We're a sick, sick country! Where the hell do they get all those fucking guns! Bobby said, he said it himself, he said maybe we're all doomed anyway. That's what he said! Christ, first Jack, then Bobby! Christ! Don't forget Martin Luther—If he dies, I'm going all the way to Australia! Christ! We're a sick society! Sick, sick! Oh, no, it can't be! I saw it all! Jesus, it didn't even sound like a gun! Not like *Gunsmoke* or *The Virginian.* Just a pop, like some Chinese firecracker down in Chinatown. I tell you it's all part of a great big plot! Dallas, Memphis, and now Los Angeles. America! Home of the brave! Home of the grave they mean! The dirty bastards, what the hell are they trying to do to us! They got him, they got him! They got the bastard who did it. Hey, turn up the sound on that TV! Hey, let's hear what's coming over the radio! Give him air, please give him air! Senator Kennedy has been shot! Senator Kennedy has been shot, is that possible? It is possible, ladies and gentlemen, it is possible, he has! Oh, God, no, it can't be again. It can't be happening here! Not here! Los Angeles. Kill him! Lynch him! Get the bastard! Slow down, slow down! If you don't slow down and be careful somebody's going to kill the bastard. Look, we don't want another Dallas! Shots! Shots! Look out, there's a madman in here and he's killing everybody! Keep him alive! Don't kill him! We want the bastard alive! What's America coming to! My God, all those kids and Ethel pregnant! My God! He can't leave us! He can't die. He doesn't need a priest! He needs a doctor! Let's not have another Dallas! Another Oswald! Another Jack Ruby! I saw him, I saw him! Those big niggers got him! They got him! Looks like a dirty little Jew! Nobody said he was a Jew! I saw him, I saw him! The guns, the guns, the guns, where do they get their fucking hands on all those fucking guns! Watch your language, sir! Look, I'm bleeding! Sir, there are ladies present! Look, I'm bleeding! My heart's busting! Sir, I'm a Republican, and I don't like it! Don't "sir" me, you Republican prick! You were an—you are an American before you were a goddamn Republican! And if you aren't bleeding, you aren't an American! Terrence, come away! Everybody's crazy! Terrence, come in! Terrence! Terrence, I'm going to shut our door! Those Democrats! They think they own the country! They think this is their country! The hell with all the nigger-loving Kennedys! You fucking, lousy Republican! Open the fucking door before I kick it down, you Republican prick! Shut up, Jim. You want to get arrested! Jim, come back in here! Jim! They're showing it again. Bobby's going to be shot again! All right, folks. Please, folks. I know how you feel, but please get back in your rooms. Let's not have any disturbance here. This is San Francisco. This is the Mark. Please, folks. Thank you, folks. Let's keep calm. All of you would do a lot better if you prayed. Poor Drysdale. What's that about Drysdale? Didn't you hear? He shut out the Pirates, 5 to 0. Yeah, but what about that Vaseline pitch? All them scoreless innings don't mean a thing. I'm from right here in San Francisco and I ought to know. The Giants scored on him in that ninth inning. He shut the Giants out. The hell he did! Drysdale whacked Dietz with the bases loaded in the ninth and that son of a bitch of an umpire said Dietz stuck his elbow in the way!

Now, when the hell did you ever hear—? Hold it down, fellers. Hold it down. Thank you. Keep praying. Good night. Good night. Good night. Jesus!

Devers heard the lullaby until sleep intercepted him just short of understanding, horror, and heartbreak. Sleep took him to the geography of dreams.

He was the bravest and noblest lad in all the world. He was Devers of Princeton, and there were thousands upon thousands in the sweep of Palmer Stadium to cheer his name. Princeton versus Yale. Devers of Princeton versus Fallon of Yale.

The scoreboard clock was running. Very late in the fourth quarter. Time running out, shadows running with the wind. An equation of zeros on the scoreboard. Princeton's ball, first down Princeton on its own twenty-five-yard line. Princeton quarterback, Jack Kennedy, called a pass play. Forrest Devers, left end, was running. Jack Fallon was running. The scoreboard clock was running. Devers faked Fallon. He was in the clear. The scoreboard clock was running. Devers was running.

He turned his head and raised his eyes as high as his dreams of glory. Out of the sky's emptiness appeared the football which Jack Kennedy had spiraled into sweet November's orbit. Devers of Princeton reached beyond his grasp with sure hands to snare the football. The whole world in his hands, he dulled blades of grass with his cleats and made for the goal line.

The sleeper was gone from the bed, the dreamer not gone from the dream. The sleeprunner hit the straight chair blocking a window high above California Street. The chair, the dream, and Devers of Princeton toppled. The chair broke. The wall below the window did not.

TWO

A stillness. Dark, familiar, foreboding.

Devers could not tell if he was awake, dreaming, alive, or dead.

He read his biological clock and sensed that dawn was not too far away. He read his palms with his thumbs and felt the sweat of life.

Awareness returned with pain. A slab of ice was crushing his head. When he brought up a hand to remove it, he touched a towel, cold and wet on his hot brow.

Beyond pain, he came to memory and to a riddle in which he had to separate reality from a dream from a nightmare.

Lateral thinking. A lateral pass. A forward pass.

He remembered. Palmer Stadium. Jack. The Princeton dream. The long pass. Miles on the telephone. *Dad! Kennedy's been shot!* Other voices, violence's voice in the corridor. Bobby. Bobby was shot. Not Jack. Not Dallas. Not 1963. Bobby. Los Angeles. 1968. June. Now.

Ah, Christ. Ah, Christ.

Devers searched the dark. No straight chair where the straight chair had been placed. No toppled chair where the toppled chair should have been. No Jack Daniel's bottle on the other bed. No telephone. The night table. The telephone.

Devers shut his eyes, but not for long. Fear opened them. He was not alone in the room. Someone or something was in another corner of the dark.

He turned his heavy head and eyes in the direction of the door to the corridor. It was shut. Unlocked. Unbolted. Sleep-runners feared windows, not doors.

He turned to the windows. No cry of agony, no groan, no whimper, only stabs at his heart and bowels.

A ghost. Death, familiar Death, with the familiar beard. Seated in the upholstered chair. Jake the Jew. Jacob Wald.

Devers faced the ghost of his grandfather and communicated with him in silence, the language of ghosts.

Grandpa, what's happened? Is Bobby dead? Is Bobby dying? Am I dead? Am I dying?

The ghost coughed.

Miles, say something. Who's dead? Who's alive? Cough!

The ghost walked on long legs. Water ran. The ghost was upon Devers. Hot towel off, cold towel on. Eye to eye, silence to silence.

Devers watched his son return to the chair before he shut his eyes and opened his mind to the riddle of silence.

What does Miles' beard hide that neither darkness nor silence can hide? The presence of a young mourner at a wake. And what does the beard reveal that neither light nor voice can reveal? Its own correctness. Mourning becomes the old, not the young.

Whose wake is it? Sweet America's? Bobby's? Mag's? Karen's? Mine?

Who rules the silence? God? Miles? Is there a mathematics of silence with quantity, measure, property, and relation? Is there a geography of silence with subsurfaces of dreams and nightmares and hallucinations? What is the name of the silence between Miles and me? What is its meaning? Is it the silence that is the highest form of attention? The silence that answers the dead? The silence that keens for the dead?

Out of questions, out of his mind, Devers no longer read the silence. He read the photograph of Jack and himself.

He saw through it and unburied from the frame the folded, forgotten poem.

Must the bugles blow? / Doesn't the wind blow cold? / Must the drums be muffled? / Doesn't the casket choke the flag? / Must the rifles crack? / Isn't heartbreak enough? / Must the cannon roar? / Aren't tears loud enough? / Must history repeat itself? / God, wasn't Christ enough?

Devers decided it was not a poem, not worth remembering. It had no meaning save in the remembrance of the forgotten, of the blocked, the hidden. Hidden by the boy hiding—

The silence screamed Miles' answer. Miles' warning.

Requiescat in pace alava sholem farewell frank merriwell.

The boy hiding within him was dead. The boy had ceased to speak to him. The shape of Forrest Devers' life was broken, and there was nothing more to be said.

ABOUT THE AUTHOR

George Zuckerman's first novel was THE LAST FLAPPER. Born in Brooklyn, a University of South Carolina graduate, and a World War II veteran, he was a newspaperman, short story writer, and screenwriter. He has a son and daughter and lives with his wife in Santa Monica, California.